FAE'S FATE
FATED MATES OF THE FAE ROYALS, SUMMER COURT BOOK 7
HELEN WALTON

Walton House Publishing

WALTON HOUSE PUBLISHING

CONTENTS

FOREWORD

AUTHOR NOTE
Choosing character names is not always easy, and there are times you pick them to mean something for the character and the story. I've included the pronunciation and meaning of the names, and if you're like me, and like to know and still pronounce the names the way you read them, then welcome to my club.

Niamh pronounced neeve meaning radiance.

Fintan pronounced fin-tan meaning white fire.

Eamon pronounced aim-on meaning keeper of riches.

Maeve pronounced may-veh meaning intoxicating.

Diarmuid pronounced deer-mid meaning without enemy.

Orlaith pronounced or-lah meaning golden princess.

Rian pronounced ree-an means little king.

Briana pronounced bree-a-nah meaning noble.

Aislinn pronounced ash-lin meaning a vision or dream.

Saoirse pronounced seer-sha meaning freedom.

Lorcan pronounced lor-can meaning silent or fierce.

Ciara pronounced kee-ra meaning dark.

Roisin pronounced row-sheen meaning little rose.

Donagh pronounced done-acka meaning brown-haired warrior.

Deirdre pronounced deer-dree meaning broken-hearted.

Malachi pronounced mal-lah-key means messenger of God.

Fallon pronounced fa-len meaning descended from a ruler.

Ailbhe pronounced all-bay meaning white.

Tadhg pronounced tie-guh meaning poet or philosopher.

Eabha pronounced ey-ya meaning life.

For in the darkest moments of
love the message is clear.

CHAPTER ONE

CIARA

ONE WOULD THINK I'D be nervous about going to Earth for the first time. I wasn't. Deep inside, where little eddies would circle my stomach whenever nerves arose, there was nothing but calm. I'd packed my travel cases with clothes and books from my bedchambers inside the palace. I spun slowly in a small circle, taking in the bed made from the silvery wood of the tallest trees in the Summer Court. Pale yellow sheets and pillows decorated the mattress. Rugs woven into the shape of flowers in delicate golden hues lined the timber floor. My sister Roisin's paintings of the library hung on the walls. She understood my favorite place was the library. I'd live there if it was possible, but being a princess meant I had to live in the palace and protect the Spring of Life as was our duty as a Fae royal.

An inadequate job we'd performed of late. The spring had almost ceased to flow. Father, the Fae King, had on the sly been using his powers to keep our magic spring alive, and now he was suffering the consequences of his actions. My brother's mate was a witch, and she'd made Father a sleeping potion to ease his decline. We'd failed to see Father's deterioration because we were too focused on searching for a cure. I spun again before tears welled in my eyes, recalling Father lying so still in his bed. My focus went back to what I might need on this trip. I'd packed everything. Considering I had two travel cases the size of me, and one was full of my most prized books, what else might I need?

A cure to our spring's problems.

A way for Father to live.

For all of us to live.

Nodding my head, I promised myself I would be the one to find the cure. I'd searched for years, but that didn't mean I wouldn't find a cure. Each book I'd read meant I was one book closer to finding what we needed. I swung a cape around my shoulders. My other sister, Aislinn, said Ireland was cold, and we needed to look like we were human to fit in with the town. We'd never fit in with our flower crowns in our hair. Plus, the seamstresses in the Summer Court made our clothes from the finest Fae materials. My yellow dress shimmered in the sunlight streaming in through the windows as though made from the beams of light themselves.

So at odds with my power over the shadows and darkness. Sometimes I chose lighter colored dresses to alleviate the way I'd *feel* dark too. Other times I worked with the mood and dressed in navy blue and black dresses, much to my mother's despair. My siblings always complained when I snuck up on them, but I didn't always do it on purpose. My powers seemed to escape on their own and cover me in shadows, concealing my presence. It had made for an enjoyable time when I was younger, creeping up on all my older siblings. I'd learned a lot because of my sneaky ways, too.

I left my bedchambers after setting my bags by the door for collection and walked along the marble hallways. My bare feet padded without a sound. There was no one to sneak up on, though. Everyone was with Father, watching over him. Well, they had been when I'd left to pack. Perhaps they'd left too. We couldn't sit around and do nothing while he was dying.

"Ciara!" Malachi, my best friend, called out to me as he turned into the same hallway I was walking along. "I found something."

A beautiful smile graced his face as he came closer to me. He held up a brown leather-bound book, hands shaking a little with his excitement.

I rushed toward him, my calm stomach giving a little jump at the sight of Malachi as I clasped the edges of the book. "What?"

"What's wrong?" he asked, his smile dropping and his strawberry blonde eyebrows tugging inward as he frowned.

I shook my head, swallowed the emotions building in my throat, and whispered, "Father."

Malachi placed his warm hand on top of mine. "What about him?"

I nodded toward the closest door, which led into our library in the palace. No matter where I went, books surrounded me. Malachi opened the door, and we slipped inside, shutting the solid timber door behind us. Thankfully, the room was empty. I slumped onto a settee. Malachi joined me and tapped his knee into mine, sending a tingle of awareness through my limb that I shouldn't have for my friend.

"Tell me," he said, more of a question than a demand from my closest friend.

I drew in a deep breath. "Father has been feeding his power into the spring and it's killing him."

His sapphire blue eyes widened. His sensual lips parted, but no words fell out. Then his arms wrapped around me, and he drew me into a comforting hug.

"I'm so sorry, Ciara," he whispered into my ear.

"Me too," I whispered back, sensing the tears building in my eyes. I drew back and opened the book he'd given me because I needed to be strong. I needed to find a cure to help Father. "What should I read?"

He flicked through the book and pointed at a drawing. It was a picture of a pillar with a face carved into the stone.

"Do you think this is what Rian and Sophia saw at the top of the waterfall in Crystal Creek?"

"I'm guessing yes, but we'd have to ask them. They're in Mother's and Father's bedchambers."

"They're not in the Amazon jungle?"

"Everyone is here."

My eldest brother Rian had found his fated mate Sophia on a trip to Earth while searching for a cure for our problems. Sophia was a jaguar shifter and the queen of her people. They spent most of their time in the jungle now.

"Let's go ask them."

"You can. I'm leaving."

"You're leaving?"

I nodded. "I'm going to Earth. Aislinn and her newfound fated mate Fallon discovered the location where our Spring of Life connects the two worlds."

"This is incredible news." Malachi stood with his excitement, then noticed I wasn't as thrilled as I should be.

"It is, but it won't fix our problems. They found a secret society, too." I couldn't believe I hadn't read about them in our library. "They protect the fountain on Earth. Aislinn said they have an extensive underground library, too. They might be able to help us."

Malachi stared at me as if I'd grown taller in the space of a second, and it was impossible.

"You're going to Earth? And you weren't going to tell me?"

"I was coming to find you. We have little time. Everything is a mess." I stroked my fingers along the spine of the book. "If these humans have books that can help us, then I need to go. I'm the one who understands them."

"You're not the only one. I understand them too. I'll go with you."

"It's too dangerous." I shook my head.

"But not too dangerous for you?" He scowled and folded his arms over his chest.

"I'll have guards with me."

"Good, but I'm still going. You're my best friend. We look out for each other."

"I don't want to risk you getting hurt."

"But you'll risk me turning mortal and dying if I don't help." He huffed out an exasperated breath.

"Since you put it like that..." I stood and tucked the book under my arm. The warm leather was a familiar sensation against my skin. "Go home and pack. I'll talk to Rian and Sophia. Meet me at the tower."

He smiled. Every time I saw him smile because he'd gotten his way with me yet again made the special place in my heart for him glow. A few years ago, when the spring's problems began, Mother and Father told us to choose a mate since there'd been so few fated matings since Father locked the Veil into the Summer Court. I'd considered asking Malachi to be my mate. We were best friends, had the same interests in books, and loved each other unconditionally. I was attracted to him more than I should be for a friend. But there was always the notion in the back of my mind that one day I'd find my fated mate. I'd find the one man meant for me and me alone. When the day arrived, I wanted to be free to experience all the love that arose with a fated mate.

I'd seen the way Malachi gazed at me sometimes. The way he couldn't meet my eyes when he read sexual passages in the books. I always felt my cheeks heat when I read those books around him. There were times when my skin ignited from a brief touch of his fingers while passing books. He'd occasionally snatched his hand away as though he, too, felt it. He might not have been averse to the idea of us mating. We'd be a good couple.

"Malachi," I said, making him pause at the door. "I love you."

"I love you too." He blew me a kiss, opened the door, and strode into the marble hallway, vanishing around a corner.

If we were fated mates, we would have already had years of happiness together. Now, with the spring drying up, I might never experience the joy of having a chosen mate, let alone finding a fated mate, or the ecstasy of being with one in every way. Before the spring dried up in its entirety, I would ask Malachi to be my mate. The idea wasn't bad. It wasn't good either. When Fae marked each other, they exchanged memories, too. The problem was, I was a part of all of Malachi's memories and he was embedded in all of mine. There would be no learning anything about each other.

If I chose Malachi, then I needed to be certain. I wouldn't force him to give up on finding his fated mate, either. He deserved happiness as much as me.

I had to be certain we wouldn't save the spring.

Certain our end was near.

CHAPTER TWO
CIARA

AFTER CONFIRMING WITH RIAN and Sophia that the drawing was of the statue that had shot darts at them, I left the palace and marched to the library, because while the book had the drawing, there had been no information about what the statues were. There was a niggling sensation tugging at my brain. I was missing an important piece of information. Two and two weren't adding up to four. More like two, if I was being honest. Even that was being generous. My long dress swished around my legs with my hurried walk, but the fabric was soft and flowing, like I was barely even wearing it.

A sense of calm soothed my body as the library grew closer. Whether it was the impressive building with a spire for an entrance and the massive wings on either side or the books inside calling to my heart, I wasn't sure. I opened the teal green entrance door and ducked inside. Sunshine sparkled on the covers of the gold-foiled books in the display section. These were our most precious tomes. The ones I'd assumed would hold our secrets, but they mentioned nothing about our Spring of Life, which I'd found odd considering it was what made us who we were.

I swung right into the human section where Eabha, our ancient librarian, magicked books from Earth to our realm so we could keep up to date. If there was a library dedicated to the Fae in Ireland, why hadn't the books appeared here? I walked along the rows of carved wooden bookshelves, my fingers and brain searching for the knowledge I didn't yet know.

Eabha turned the corner of the next shelf and almost bumped into me.

"Ciara," she exclaimed, placing a hand over her heart. "I didn't hear you come in."

"Aye," I said distractedly as I perused the titles on the shelf closest to me.

"Are you looking for something in particular?"

I frowned. Was I? Why had I come here when I was leaving soon? Was it the familiarity of the place? The comfort I always experienced when surrounded by books.

"I'm not sure," I said, running a finger down the closest spine. Even touching books made me feel better. Perhaps that was it. I was worried and needed comfort. I dropped my hand and turned my attention to Eabha. "Have you ever heard of a secret society of humans who protect us?"

An infinitesimal twitch near her right eye marred the serene face she usually kept in place.

I clasped her hands in mine. "Tell me everything you understand about The Fellowship of the Infinite Spring."

"I never said I comprehend anything." She ducked her chin and avoided looking me in the eye.

"Please, Eabha, you don't realize how important this is."

"Oh, child, I do. I'm not blind." She raised her chin, meeting my searching gaze with one holding a wealth of knowledge. "I see what's happening here."

"If you see, then why haven't you said anything?"

"Why haven't you?"

I dropped my hand from her arm. "It wasn't my decision."

"The King?"

I nodded my head once. There was no point denying it. We all followed the King. He'd kept us safe for many years, but now our sanctuary was turning lethal.

"I read about them many centuries ago in a book in here." She faced the long row of shelves. "Would you believe as soon as I placed it back on the shelf, it disappeared?"

"Do you remember what it said?"

"I'm sorry." She patted my cheek. "It was so long ago. I've read so much. My mind is jumbling the words." She tapped the side of her head. "In recent times, the words are even more confusing inside me. I sometimes think the words are dying." She lowered her voice and said, "That I'll die too once they've all vanished."

The declining spring was affecting everyone in different ways. After Aislinn found her fated mate,

Fallon, and the group of Fae who we'd left on Earth by accident before the Fae King sealed the Veil, we'd seen firsthand how bad a Fae could turn when one of Fallon's group attacked them. We'd locked him in the dungeon because he'd become so volatile. Aislinn's guards complained about their powers being erratic while they were on Earth. I'd even yelled at Aislinn one time, and I'd never raised my voice toward her before.

Roisin was making strange paintings which were not her normal style. As for my other brothers and sisters, they all lived on Earth now and hadn't divulged if their powers were acting differently. I suspected they were, or they soon would be.

"Is there any information you can think of?"

"Hmm." Her brows dipped into a frown. "They're old. Older than me. I remember reading the book and thinking it was strange we didn't know about them."

"I wonder..." I paced away, then back again.

"What is running through your mind?"

"If we made them our protectors, would they also be the ones able to influence our spring? What if it's them and they want to kill us?"

Eabha sighed. "Seems doubtful to me a society designed for protection would try to kill the ones they're meant to protect."

"But our powers are acting strange. Your memories are affected. Father is..."

"Is there a problem with the King?"

"I shouldn't have come here," I said, swinging around. "We need to find out if this Fellowship is the one causing our problems or if they are trying to help and protect us."

"Ciara, wait."

"We can't wait any longer." I swept a hand around the library and said, "I've searched the books here. The answer isn't in the Summer Court."

She stepped closer to me and said, "You grew up with fear for humans, but we used to live in harmony with them."

"Are you saying I should trust them?"

"I'm saying don't jump to conclusions with no evidence. You're smarter than that."

I dipped my head, then strode from the library. Eabha comprehended more. I was certain, but I didn't have time to pry the secrets from her muddled brain. Any other time I asked her a question, she knew the answer straight away. Were we all deteriorating? Dying? If that was the case, then I needed to hurry.

Lifting the length of my dress, I ran as fast as I could, following the path through the fields until I arrived at the tower housing the doorway to the Veil. Many guards stood surrounding the place. Their expressions made me slow my steps. I spotted Malachi talking to the guard nearest the tower, no not a guard, a scribe.

I rushed up to them. "Are you ready?"

"Princess." The scribe bobbed his head. "The doorway is unpassable."

"Ridiculous."

His lips pursed. "I assure you, it is not. When the guards opened the door to check the sudden surge of power coming from inside, we almost lost them to the turbulence of the Veil. I have never seen the Veil so disrupted. It doesn't want to be contained. It wants free like a lot of us. I'm afraid the torrent inside the tower will rip you to shreds."

"But we have to leave."

"I'm sorry."

Darkness swarmed my entire body, covering me from head to foot. Raw power thrummed from my palms.

"Ciara." Malachi's voice penetrated the thick rush of power. A bright white light shone from his hands as he wielded his power and lunged into the shadows. His hands found my shoulders, and he drew me into his embrace. "Breathe. Relax."

I shuddered. What was wrong with me? Drawing in a steadying breath, I hauled the shadows back until the darkness surrounding me dissipated.

"There you are."

"I'm here." I tipped up my chin to stare into his blue eyes. "Thank you."

"I'll always find you. No matter how dark it is."

I smiled. "Because you'll manipulate the light."

He smiled and shrugged. I squeezed him briefly, then stepped out of his embrace.

"If we can't use the doorway, what do we do?"

"Simple," Aislinn said.

I snapped my head her way, having not noticed her and Fallon's approach while the darkness consumed me. I'd always struggled with my power. Mother was pregnant with me when the Trappers burned her at the stake and almost killed her. Almost killed me too before I was even born. It was like the night had left darkness inside me. Perhaps this was why my powers commanded the shadows.

"How so?" I asked.

"We're Fae royals. We'll make our doorway." Aislinn twirled one of her daggers around in her fingers.

"I've never been through the Veil."

"So you shouldn't," Aislinn said in her big sister's voice.

I narrowed my eyes at Aislinn. She slid the dagger into a holster, then lifted her hands. Power coated her palms, making the area around her glow a beautiful shade of purple. Since my power was darkness, my hands didn't glow a beautiful color. They developed shadows. Darkness. I doubted if I called on the Veil, it would look pretty the way Aislinn was making it part for us.

"Ready?" she asked, then swung her head to the side. "Erin, what are you doing here?"

"Is Fallon's sister coming too?" I asked as she appeared, twisting her hands in a nervous gesture.

"No, Erin is staying here," Fallon said.

Erin flung her arms around Fallon and hugged him. "Be safe."

"I will," he said. "You realize I can protect myself."

"Yes, but you're my only family."

Fallon nodded, then clasped Aislinn's hand.

Erin stepped closer to us. "I'm Fallon's sister."

"Ciara, Aislinn's sister, and this is Malachi."

Malachi held out his hand. Erin placed hers in his.

"Pleasure to meet you," Malachi said.

A small smile tugged at the edges of her lips. They stared at each other as though caught in a haze.

"Sorry, time to go," I said, tugging Malachi's other hand.

"Have we met before?" Malachi asked.

"No," she said.

"I feel like..." he trailed off. "Never mind. I'll see you around."

"Sure," Erin said.

I tugged Malachi toward the Veil, even more eager to leave the Summer Court. We stepped beside Aislinn and Fallon. Aislinn gave me a questioning glance, but I shook my head. I wasn't sure what had happened, but I didn't like it. Malachi never looked at other women. He probably did, but he never did it when he was with me.

I didn't like the way my chest hurt when he stared at Erin. I hated the way my power had surged to the surface when he'd touched her.

If he wasn't my best friend, then I'd say he was my fated mate by my reaction. It was probably because we were best friends. Born on the same day, we'd grown up together, safe inside the Summer Court.

Now we were venturing into the unknown. At least he was by my side on this epic journey. I'd always imagined Malachi being by my side, but I hadn't factored in what would happen when we found our fated mates. With the way Malachi had gazed at Erin, perhaps he'd found his today.

CHAPTER THREE
MALACHI

A STEADY POUNDING HAMMERED inside my head. I tore my gaze away from the new Fae in the Summer Court. Erin. There was something about her, but I couldn't put my finger on it. I'd always lived inside the Summer Court, so I'd never met her before because from what I'd learned from Ciara about the newcomers, all of them had only lived on Earth.

The Veil shimmered around me. Magic pulsed against my skin. I'd never been inside the Veil. Never been taught how to access the magic of the Veil since the King had locked the curtain separating Earth and the Summer Court before I was born. Ciara's fingers squeezed mine. The connection between us was always there. She was my best friend. When I lifted my gaze back to the swirling energy around us, the scene before my eyes was a new one.

Instead of the familiarity of the place I called home, a land of extensive green stretched far ahead of us. The guards stepped from the Veil, checking the surroundings before ushering us out. Aislinn and Fallon walked out of the Veil with a confidence I wished I had. Ciara's fingers tightened on mine. At least she was nervous, too. We'd be nervous together. I squeezed her hand, too. She raised her chin and squared her shoulders. Trust Ciara to put on a brave face. She only ever let me see the other side of her. I was the luckiest man alive. I'd had her all to myself since the day I was born. But now everything was changing.

Now I'd have to share her with her fated mate.

If she was like her brothers and sisters, then I believed she'd find him on this trip to Earth. They'd all found theirs a short time ago on Earth. Why wouldn't she find hers, too?

I wanted her to be happy, but I was selfish in wanting her to be happy with me. I loved her more than she understood. More than I'd ever told her. When her parents had requested she and her siblings choose a mate, I'd thought she'd choose me, but she hadn't. I recognized deep down she longed for her fated mate. The one all Fae yearned for.

Except me. I'd give mine up in a heartbeat to be with Ciara.

I stepped through the shimmering magic of the Veil onto the spongy green grass of Ireland. A light drizzling rain fell onto my face like the wings of a butterfly tickling my skin. The Veil closed behind us, taking the magic of the Summer Court with it.

"How do we access the Veil?"

"You can't. Only the royal family can unlock it enough for us to slip through," Aislinn said.

"So, if I'm separated from you, then I'm stuck here?"

"As if you'd become separated from Ciara. You two have been joined at the hip since birth." She rolled her eyes.

She had a point, but we didn't comprehend what would happen on Earth. I sure didn't since I'd never come here.

"Can Ciara work the Veil?"

Ciara shot me a glare. "Of course I can."

"Since when?" Aislinn asked.

"Saoirse taught me. Lorcan too." She crossed her arms over her chest.

The drizzling rain landed on her eyelashes, turning them into a magical, glowing image I'd keep in my head forever. My gaze dipped to her lips, glistening in the rain. Dia, I wanted to kiss her. So many times, I'd imagined what it'd be like. What we'd be like together as a couple instead of friends.

"Those two are sneaky," Aislinn said.

I tore my gaze away from my best friend and focused on our surroundings. A forest stretched beside us. Tall, bright green moss-covered trunks made the path into the forest glow in the dim daylight. Gray clouds hung heavy in the air and drifted down the hill to the village in the distance. Colored buildings popped amongst the greenery of the place. On the other side of the village lay a stormy blue-gray ocean.

"The society is at the end of the village. We must walk through the village to get to it," Fallon said. "Aislinn, did you get the coats and hats made in time?"

Aislinn nodded and motioned for the guard to drop the travel case in his hand. She opened the lid and hauled out two long coats, handed one to Ciara, and put the other one on herself.

"It's cold here and humans look at people if they're not wearing the right clothes for the weather," Fallon said.

Aislinn tugged a woven hat onto her head and then laughed as she wriggled the other one onto Ciara's head. Her pretty crown of flowers disappeared, but I knew that if the hat knocked a few flowers from her hair, they'd regrow in an instant. I'd stored one of her fallen flowers in a glass jar in a drawer in my bedchambers just to have a piece of her near me at night.

"People don't have flower crowns either," Fallon said.

"Makes sense to fit in." I tugged on the bottom of my shirt. It was an off-white shade of Fae material lined with gold buttons. "What about us?"

"We'll do." Fallon nodded. "Once the guards stow their swords in the travel cases."

"There's no room in mine," Ciara said.

"Yours weigh a ton," Emer, one of Ciara's guards, said.

"It's full of books." Ciara shrugged.

"We're going to a library to look at books," Aislinn said. "Why would you bring books with you?"

"To cross reference," Ciara and I said at the same time. We both laughed.

Aislinn shook her head.

"Here," Fallon said, "stow the swords in this case. Now the coats are no longer in there."

Aislinn's guards, Brogan and Conlan, did so, as did Ciara's guards, Emer and Ivo.

"Right, we'll head there now. Remember, these humans are helping us," Fallon said. "Which means no using your powers around them unless necessary."

"Are everyone's powers acting weird?" I asked.

"We're not sure," Aislinn said.

I hadn't used mine, but Ciara's were not right with the way her shadows had engulfed her at the tower.

"Lead the way, since you recognize where we're going."

Brogan and Conlan marched down the hill. Aislinn and Fallon followed. We followed behind them, and Emer and Ivo followed behind us. The trek down the hillside was as quiet as walking in the Summer Court. Birds flew across the sky in a flock, heading in the same direction as us. The rain eased and then stopped, leaving us with damp clothes, but Fae didn't suffer from the cold, so it didn't bother us.

We walked into the town and found humans everywhere. I'd never met one, neither had Ciara. They appeared the same as us, apart from their clothes. They wore thick coats, making their limbs appear twice the size. Most also wore boots, while we were barefoot. I supposed shoes would have helped us fit in better, but we hurried along the streets until we arrived at a wall at the end of the village.

Without warning, the wall shifted as a door opened and a man with a thick gray beard stepped through it.

"You're back," he said, nodding at Aislinn and Fallon. "And you've brought others."

"This is my sister Ciara, who I mentioned is the scholar. Her friend Malachi is also likewise inclined. And her two guards, Emer and Ivo," Aislinn said.

"Come in." He stepped aside and waved at the entrance. "I'm Alister."

We walked through the doorway and Alister closed the heavy wooden door behind us. I scanned the area, taking in the unkempt garden. Vines grew everywhere, strangling the plants struggling to flower under the thick masses of leaves. In the distance, the sound of trickling water gurgled, reminding me of the Spring of Life back home.

Alister stepped beside us. "Would you like to see the Infinite Spring?"

"I'd like to see the library," Ciara said.

I couldn't agree with her more. Seeing the corresponding spring here on Earth wouldn't give us any answers. I derived answers from words. Books housed those words. Books were where we'd find the answers.

CHAPTER FOUR

CIARA

I WAS SO GLAD Malachi had offered to come with me to Earth. When we'd walked through the village all those humans stared at us, they'd made chills run down my spine. I'd read the stories of the olden days when we used to live in harmony with them, but I'd also read the stories of the Trappers and how they'd attempted to kill us all. How they'd believed burning us alive would release our powers to them. I shuddered at the image, knowing they had burned my mother, Aislinn, and Briana. How they'd kill both sets of my grandparents before I was born.

I wasn't sure what to think about humans. There was a part of me who wanted the peace we once had, and there was a part of me who wanted to hide in the safety of the Summer Court. Father had only kept us safe by locking us inside. The problems we were facing were catastrophic, but we'd had centuries of happiness.

Alister led the way through the garden. I shoved aside the tall plants to follow him, eager to see the library. The books held so many secrets. My fingers itched to open them. Pry the words from the pages and absorb them into my mind.

No one but Malachi understood my excitement for reading books.

I stepped into a rose bush having not seen it amongst the other overgrown plants. Thorns stuck into the coat and ripped the material, scratching my leg.

"Ow," I mumbled.

"Hold still," Malachi said.

He bent and tenderly tugged the offending limb from my clothes sending a skittering of goose bumps up my leg and held the rose bush limb back for me to find a safe way out of my ridiculous predicament. How did I get myself into such a mess? Alister and everyone else seemed to find their way through the garden without mishap. Once I was clear, Malachi let go of the branch and it snapped back into place, hiding amongst the overgrown plants yet again. The Fellowship had booby-trapped the area with vegetation to keep people away. Briana would enjoy this place and using her powers over plants, she'd make the place shine like the gardens back home.

A home we might not even be able to get back to if we didn't fix the spring.

Alister lit a lantern I hadn't noticed him carrying and said, "Down we go."

Then he disappeared. I rushed forward, scared he'd fallen but beyond the thick bush was a set of stairs leading underground.

"The library is underground," Aislinn said.

"Great."

Malachi and I had once found a cave in the Summer Court, and I'd been so scared about being sealed inside and having my dark powers overcome me. That they would consume me and all I'd know was darkness that we'd never mentioned it to anyone. Only my best friend comprehended my fears.

Aislinn, Fallon, and her guards followed Alister down the stairs. They made it look easy. Below appeared well-lit, but the entire idea of being underground made my skin crawl in a bad way.

"Are we going in?" Ivo asked.

"Go ahead," Malachi said. "We'll be right behind you."

"But our job is to protect the princess."

"The garden has a wall around it. I doubt anyone will come and hurt her," Malachi said. "Besides, we'll only be a minute."

A minute in Fae time or human time? There was a big difference.

Ivo scowled. "I don't like it, but we'll wait at the bottom of the stairs."

Malachi nodded, waited for them to disappear then hugged me.

"Everything is all right, Ciara, you can do this."

I shook my head. "I don't think I can. It's underground. You remember what happened at the cave."

"We were children then. You're a grown Fae now, besides think of all the books waiting for you down there."

I cocked my head to the side. "There is that. But what if the walls collapse? And buried us alive?"

"The walls won't collapse."

"How do you know?"

"I do." He eased me away from the warmth of his chest.

I missed the contact at once. The way his strong arms held me. How he'd eased my fear by his comforting hug, and the way my skin tingled from his hands holding me.

"But how?"

His lips tilted to the side on the right with the lopsided smile he always reserved for me when my questions amused him.

"We both read books about caves and underground structures after your panic attack."

"Logic doesn't come in here." I placed my hands on my hips the strange sensation tingling my skin forgotten now he wasn't touching me.

"If the walls collapsed, I'd find you. I'd find you anywhere."

I lowered my hands and clasped his needing contact with him again. "Stay by my side."

"Always."

"If I have a panic attack, can you carry me out?"

He chuckled. "You won't have a panic attack, but yes, I'll carry you out if you need me to."

I stretched up on my tiptoes and kissed his cheek as I had many times over the past but this time my lips tingled at the brush against his skin. I drew back and said, "You're the best friend ever."

His lopsided smile fell from his face, and I wanted it back. What did I say to make it go away?

"Malachi?"

"Hmm?"

Was he experiencing these strange sensations too? Or was it because we were on Earth, and everything felt different?

"Don't worry about it."

He frowned. "What do you want to ask?"

I couldn't possibly ask him if he was attracted to me. It would be a strange thing to ask my best friend.

"Nothing." I placed one foot in front of the other, shoved the strange stirrings in my body aside, and stepped down the first stair.

At least there were rows of bright white torches lighting our way down the staircase.

"I understand you better, so what was it?" he asked as he stepped down the stairs beside me.

We reached the bottom of the stairs, and I lifted my chin. The sight before me was one of an immense library. Bigger than the library back home. Rows upon rows of bookshelves stretched for hundreds of feet. So many books lined the shelves I'd be here for centuries and never read them all. I'd believed our library in the Summer Court held every book but perhaps I was mistaken. In the center of the underground library was a long wooden table running the length of the room. People sat at the table, every one of them with an open book before them.

"Wow." I breathed out the word on an exhale.

Malachi followed my line of sight and said, "I agree."

CHAPTER FIVE
MALACHI

THE SUMMER COURT LIBRARY was magical. Special. Flowering trees flourished inside the building as though they were making the books themselves, but here... here magic hummed from the books. I curled my fingers into my palms to stop them from touching the nearest book. We didn't have time for me to read every book here, but one day when we had the time, for I was sure we'd find a cure to our problems then I'd come back here and read every word on every page. My brain hungered for the knowledge waiting to be read in so many tomes.

Ciara touched her fingertips against her temple.

"You're safe," I whispered. "Look around. There are many lights, so you won't get trapped."

She nodded and stepped forward. Her sister talked with their leader animatedly which made hope flare even brighter inside me. I was such a fool sometimes for always believing in good. I wanted to believe these people were good too.

"Where do we start?" Ciara asked.

Alister motioned to the table. "We've found several books with water magic referenced in them."

"Good," Ciara said, sliding onto the bench seat and picking up a book. Her fear of being underground was forgotten now she'd focused on the pages before her. "How much have you read?"

Alister shrugged. "Passages here and there. You see how many books are in the library."

"No one has read them all?" I asked sliding onto the bench seat beside Ciara.

"No," Alister said. "There is no way a human would read all these books in one lifetime."

"Perhaps," I said picking up a book and opening it. "How did they all get here?"

"They were here long before I was alive. I couldn't say how long they've been here, to be honest. While there is a lot of information here, none of it pertains to our Fellowship. But then there is the..."

I lifted my head. "Where are your books then?"

"An excellent question. Come with me."

Ciara stood at the same time as me, our arms brushed sending a flare of awareness through my body. It was easier to keep my attraction to her locked down whenever I hugged her because I was always thinking about not letting it show, but accidental touches were different. They set my body alight with a need to devour her in passion. I shoved those thoughts back down into the depths of my repressed feelings for my best friend. We followed Alister along the length of the library until we arrived at the end.

Before us stood a bookshelf. There was no difference in the way it appeared to all the other bookshelves. They'd made it from wood. The shelves housed many volumes of books. They appeared the same as everything else.

"Watch," he said.

He drew a book from the shelf. In the blink of an eye, the entire row of books disappeared from the shelf.

"Where did they go?"

"Beats me."

I leaned forward and ran a hand along the bookshelf half expecting the books to be there to touch and that magic had made them invisible, but my hand met nothing but air. The books had vanished.

"What was in those books?"

"I couldn't tell you. We never get to read them."

"How?" Ciara asked.

"Every time we take one book the rest disappear." He turned the book, so we read the cover. The Enchantment of Water Sorcery.

"This happens often?"

"As long as I've been a member of the Fellowship. Before then, I'd say. Most likely forever."

"I don't understand," I said. "How does it keep happening if the books disappear when you take one?"

"That's the even more magical part." Alister smiled. "Watch."

A woman handed him a book. The Life Cycle of Bees. He placed it on the shelf. The magic refilled the shelves with books in an instant.

Ciara gasped. I blinked away my surprise.

"What happens if you put back the book you took from the shelf?"

"Nothing. The book stays there by itself."

Ciara stepped closer to the bookshelf and ran a hand along the spines. "They're all magical titles, but the one you put there was a human book, wasn't it?"

"Yes." Alister rubbed his hands together.

"Are you able to read the books you take?"

"Yes. Some we have to translate the languages, but we get there in the end."

I stepped beside Ciara and read the spines. There were so many I longed to take down and read, but if I removed one, they'd all disappear. Luckily the one Alister had taken was relevant to our search.

"Do the same books come back?"

"No. Every time we take one book an entire collection of new books appears. We have to choose carefully." He frowned and then glanced at the book in his hand. "I hope I've chosen correctly this time. We've lost a good number of books we've wanted to read."

"Can't you take more than one book?" Ciara asked.

"No. The books won't budge if you try to remove more than one at a time."

"It's a trading system," I said. "But who are you trading with?"

"Now this is the million-dollar question," Alister said.

"Someone is gatekeeping the knowledge and feeding it to you pieces at a time." I turned around. "Are all the books in the library here from this shelf?"

"We don't know," Alister said. "Any time we write anything down about us, the words on the pages vanish as though the ink is invisible, and we didn't write anything at all. It's no wonder no one knows about us."

"Whoever it is, they're going to a lot of trouble."

"Perhaps it's not much trouble for them?" Ciara spun around. "They would need potent magic to work all this." She peered back down the long library and touched her fingers against her temple. "Stronger than our magic."

"Different magic," I said. "Ours is based in the elements."

"Yes, your powers help Earth and now it's struggling without you."

"We've never even visited Earth. Never had the chance to. Let alone the chance to help," I said.

"Malachi?" Ciara whispered. "I need..."

She swayed on her feet.

I swept her up into my arms and hurried toward the stairs and the exit.

"I've got you," I whispered.

CHAPTER SIX
CIARA

"**W**HAT'S WRONG WITH CIARA?" Aislinn's voice drifted to me as though I was under water, garbled, muted, and distorted.

I squeezed my eyes shut, so I didn't have to see the worry on her face as Malachi carried me from the library. If I had full function right now, I'd be embarrassed, but the panic swirling inside me made nothing else matter.

My body jolted as Malachi marched up the stairs. His chest was firm against me. Warm. His heart beat steadily. The sound comforted me. I snuggled closer to him, letting his mere presence soothe me. Ground me. The unusual tingle in my skin started again taking me further away from the panic attack and into the desire building for my best friend.

Cool air whipped my hair around my face. I risked opening my eyes and found Malachi's jaw clenched into a hard line. He had the most perfect jaw. Solid with angles I longed to kiss, but we were best friends, and kissing was a no-no.

The soothing cadence of running water penetrated the last of my panic attack. Letting it free from its hold, I clung tighter to him and pretended for a moment I could kiss him. Then Malachi set my legs on the ground, but he kept a steady hand on my lower back to keep me from falling over. The tingles vibrated across my lower back and made me desire him even more.

"How are you doing there?"

"Better," I said, drawing in a lungful of the fresh night air. "Where are we?"

"The fountain would be my guess."

"Yes, it is," Aislinn said joining us. "Care to tell me what happened?"

I brushed strands of hair away from my face needing a moment to squash the lust building in me for my best friend. Was I the only one feeling this way? I'd felt moments like this occasionally over the years, but here on Earth, they were frequent. Was it this realm or the disruption in the spring making me feel this way? I let out a sigh since my sister was waiting for an explanation.

"I had a panic attack."

"Since when do you have panic attacks?" She folded her arms over her chest.

"For as long as I can remember. I don't like caves. They make my skin crawl and then I can't breathe. It all builds up. I feel the sense the walls are closing in on me. That the darkness of my power will consume me." I shuddered.

"Dia, Ciara, why didn't you say anything all these years?"

"It wasn't an issue back home. I made sure I wasn't anywhere that would set me off... well most of the time I suppose." The wind whipped my hair again making me wonder if it was Aislinn's power over wind causing the disturbance. Was she acting differently like me?

Aislinn brushed my hair back from my face. "How are you going to study the books in the underground library?"

"I'll be fine in a minute to go back down."

"But what if you have another attack?"

"Malachi will carry me out. He knows what to do."

Aislinn's sharp gaze landed on Malachi.

"Why didn't you tell me about Ciara's panic attacks?"

"It's her place to tell you."

Aislinn scowled harder.

"He's my best friend, Aislinn. Don't take it out on him."

I'd defend him no matter what. I'd defend him in the middle of a panic attack if he needed me to. There wasn't anything I wouldn't do for him.

"What other secrets are you two keeping?"

We exchanged glances and laughed.

"You're as bad as Saoirse and Lorcan." Aislinn huffed. "Those two were terrible for keeping their secrets."

Saoirse and Lorcan were the closest of all of us siblings. We all loved each other, but sometimes family weren't the ones you confided in. I'd always been closest to Malachi. He was more than family to me. These strange sensations I was having around him now made it hard to talk to him about them. Anything else and I would have asked him, but this... what if I ruined our friendship because the declining spring was affecting us and that was all?

"Remember when Father caught them eavesdropping..." Aislinn paused and pursed her lips. "You were maybe too young."

I recalled the moment she was talking about, but remembering Father this way made me remember he was dying, and it made me sadder than I'd ever been in my life. Aislinn's sullen expression appeared she was recalling the way Father was lying unconscious too.

I twirled the long length of my hair around my hand keeping it in place against the blowing wind and wishing I'd braided my hair the way Aislinn always did.

"I remember the time the cooks chased them from the kitchen when they stole freshly baked cakes before they had a chance to even decorate them."

"Oh yes." Aislinn attempted to smile, but it fell short. She squinted back at the way we'd come. "I should head back to the books."

"We'll be there soon. I need another minute out here."

Aislinn nodded and made her way through the thick plant life and into the shadows of the night.

I turned my attention to the fountain before us. Water cascaded from the structure and tumbled down to the cobblestones underneath, soaking into the thick moss and disappearing. Powerful magic hummed from the water. I was even calmer here and all lingering traces of the panic attack vanished. My power felt calmer too so why did the tingling sensation in my skin still run over me?

"This place is almost the same as the atrium back home."

"If the plants had overgrown the atrium." Malachi smiled.

"Did you ever imagine there was a place on Earth like ours and we'd find it?"

"Yes. We'll find everything we need," Malachi said. "I believe in us."

"I do too."

"Are you ready to head back to the library?"

"I think so. Thank you for carrying me out of there."

"Any time." He smiled. "Have you gazed up?"

"What?" I lifted my chin.

The night glittered with thousands of starlit jewels in the ebony sky. Twinkling and sparkling as though powered by magic themselves. The moon was a tiny sliver of light curved into a crescent. I imagined curling into the arc and snuggling the moonbeams to survey the beauty of the stars from amongst them.

"It's breathtaking," I said on a breathy exhale for the beauty of the Earth's sky took my breath away.

"Aye," Malachi agreed. "It would be a shame to lose it."

I lowered my gaze to his handsome face. Even with the limited light from the night sky, he took my breath away too. He tilted his head to the side and my heart leaped as anticipation built between us. Was he thinking about kissing me? Or was it the strange feelings I was experiencing being on Earth? Was he having them too? His head inched closer.

My breath caught in my lungs. Every inch of my body vibrated in anticipation of his kiss.

And then a scream rang through the air shattering the moment of attraction.

CHAPTER SEVEN
MALACHI

H AD I ALMOST KISSED my best friend? I jerked away from her before she scolded me for crossing the line of friendship. I could never lose her. No matter how much I wanted her. How much my body throbbed with the incessant need to have her under me.

"Stay here," I said.

"No, I'm going with you." Ciara pursed her lips and tilted her chin.

She was so stubborn. And infuriating sometimes. Her guards rushed forward. I'd forgotten they were with her. They must have followed us out of the library when I'd carried Ciara out, but I'd been too worried about helping her overcome her panic attack to care about anything else. Had they seen how close I'd come to kissing her? I could kick myself for getting carried away with the enchantment of the moment beneath the moonlit sky and how beautiful she'd looked. But then she was always beautiful.

"Stay with us," Emer said. "We'll protect you."

There were no other sounds apart from the woman's scream. What had happened? Did I get Ciara out of the library in time to save her from an evil we didn't understand? Why was Earth so precarious for the Fae to visit?

Ciara tapped her fingers on her crossed arms. "Well, someone has to find out what the scream was about. We can't stay here and wonder."

"I can't hear any fighting sounds," Ivo said. "It's our duty to protect you so we should stay here where we know it's safe."

"People don't scream for no reason," Ciara said.

"Do you hear any more screams?" I asked.

"No." She shook her head. "My sister is in there. If something bad is happening, then I need to help her."

I raised my eyes skyward and hauled in a centering breath. "We all go together."

The guards argued but there wasn't any point in us staying out here debating about helping. If they needed help, then we'd help. It was simple. I wouldn't run and hide, and neither would Ciara unless it was necessary. First, we needed to find out what we were dealing with.

The three of us formed a circle around Ciara as best we could. Another guard would have been preferable, so they'd protect her from all sides, but I recognized she would use her powers to protect herself if needed. But after the way they'd flared from her without her control back in the Summer Court, it wasn't the best thing for her to use her powers right now. We inched forward, closer to the library entrance.

The lights were still on. Excited voices echoed below. I raised a questioning eyebrow at Ciara. She shrugged. It didn't sound like anything nefarious was happening in the library. So why would a woman scream?

We inched down the stairs at a snail's pace placing one foot in front of the other and not making a sound. Then we'd catch whoever was down here by surprise.

But as we arrived at the end of the staircase, we found nothing amiss. The people were still sitting at the table or browsing the bookshelves. Apart from Alister and his daughter Fiona who were talking energetically with a young man. I couldn't see Aislinn or Fallon. Had they harmed them?

"Alister," I called out and waved him over.

Alister lifted his head, patted the young man on the shoulder, then walked over to us.

"Why did a woman scream?"

Alister smiled. "Sorry, my daughter was over-excited to see her son again. Brandon has been away studying for years."

"Years?"

"Oh, yes. We take our training seriously. We do not allow any humans near the Infinite Spring until they've undergone extensive training, so the spring doesn't tempt them to drink from it," Alister said.

"What happens if they do?" Ciara asked.

"They become warped and power hungry."

"Like the Trappers?" I asked.

"Yes."

"I suppose now we comprehend how the Trappers started." My fingers itched to write the words down. For there to be a place other Fae could learn what had happened in the past. A way for them to avoid them in the future too.

"We have an entire section on the Trappers," Alister said as though reading my thoughts.

"One day, I'll read them but for now we must focus on the Spring's problems."

Fiona and her son walked over to us.

"Brandon, allow me the great honor of introducing you to Fae Princess Ciara."

Brandon's smile stretched across his face so far, a surge of possessiveness flared inside me.

"A pleasure to meet you," Brandon said, his voice as smooth as running water.

I peeked at Ciara. She returned his smile and tucked her hair behind her ears. Did she find him attractive? What did it matter, he was human, but the thought of her with any man made me want to carry her out of here and hide her away in the palace tower back home. I rubbed the ache in my side near my heart.

"I'm Malachi," I said, butting in before my jealousy got the better of me and the flare of my powers I sensed building in my hands escaped in a bright burst of light.

"Nice to meet you," Brandon said holding out his hand.

I placed my hand in his and my powers throbbed even harder. I had to get control of my jealousy. How would

I be when Ciara found her fated mate? I didn't want to think about it.

"And they are?" Brandon asked.

"My guards," Ciara said. "Emer and Ivo."

"We would never harm a Fae," he said.

"The King is cautious, and we can't blame him," I said.

"I suppose not," Brandon said.

"I'm getting back to the books," Ciara said, stepping away and walking toward the table.

It wasn't like me to be distrustful, but I'd never left the Summer Court and I trusted everyone back home. Here on Earth was a different matter. Here was where the Trappers almost annihilated us to extinction. Of course, I was cautious.

"I guess we'll see you around the library?"

Brandon smiled. "I'll be here helping."

He walked over to the table and sat opposite Ciara. Great, just what I needed. More of a reason to be jealous for no damn reason. What was wrong with me? I rubbed my neck and the base of my head. The pressure building there made me rush over to Ciara's side and settle beside her. The sensation eased at once because being beside her calmed me in an instant.

Aislinn and Fallon walked out of a row between the shelves looking a little sheepish. A faint pink stained both their cheeks. I'd learned newfound mates were insatiable for each other. Would Ciara be passionate with her fated mate?

Why was I torturing myself yet again? When it was me who thought of having her naked, skin glistening from the pleasure I'd given her. Those thoughts were always in my head.

CHAPTER EIGHT
CIARA

I RUBBED THE HEELS of my hands over my tired eyes. The words were blending into each other. We'd been researching for days on end with very little sleep. Alister had shown us the sleeping barracks in the library and the tight enclosed space had sent my panic spiraling into a tight band around my chest. Malachi had squeezed my hand and led me outside once again. Setting off strange tingles along my skin. He'd been my rock as always. The one constant in my life I counted on. I had to shove the unfamiliar desire aside. We'd even dozed under the stars in the garden once we were tired, our arms brushing in the way they had for years, but now the yearnings inside me for more than friendship had made the moments more intimate for me at least. Malachi was still my Malachi. My best friend.

"You should sleep," Malachi's deep voice rumbled tiredly from across the table.

"So should you."

"We can head back to the Summer Court and sleep there?"

"With the way the spring is and Father..." I swallowed the lump in my throat. "It's too risky. What if we couldn't make it back?"

"What if we're stuck here?" Malachi whispered, his gaze darting to the side as though being trapped on Earth with humans was a terrible idea.

I frowned and chewed my lip.

"Maybe we should head back?"

"I can't," I whispered. "If I see Father again the way he was when we left then I might not leave his side."

"Us sitting by his side won't help him."

"Logically I realize that, but my emotions say otherwise."

He stretched across the table and placed his hand on top of mine. The comfort was there like always, but my skin leaped into awareness at the contact.

"We'll keep going then."

I shook my head. "Neither of us is much good when we're this tired."

Malachi stretched and yawned. I couldn't help noticing the way his shirt clung to his chest. Nor the sudden pounding of lust igniting my body. I pressed my legs together against the sudden desire filling me from the inside out. Dropping my gaze, I skimmed the book before he caught me staring at him. Gazing at him with lust. Warmth infused my cheeks. I didn't dare look at Malachi again.

"There has to be somewhere else we can sleep. What about the caravans of Fallon's old troupe? Aren't they close by?"

"I suppose," I said. "But that means less time in the library."

"Ciara, stop being stubborn." He stood and dragged my hand upward tugging me to my feet and all I wanted was for him to wrap me in his arms and tell me he felt the same way I did. "Come on, let's get out of here for a few hours."

"Fine." I sighed.

We walked along the length of the library looking for Aislinn and Fallon who weren't claustrophobic like me and had slept in the barracks here. They were in an aisle removing books from the shelves and placing them on a cart.

"Did you find a good section?" I asked.

"Perhaps," Aislinn said. "There are so many books it's hard to tell."

"Aye." I rubbed my eyes again. Even the shapes of people were blurring with how tired I was.

Aislinn narrowed her eyes at me. "What's wrong with you?"

Dia, did I look bad?

"I need to sleep. We both do." I flicked my hand toward Malachi. "I can't do it here though."

She stepped closer. "Is it your claustrophobia? Your powers?"

I nodded. "Malachi remembered you saying Fallon's troupe transported their caravans here. Are they still nearby?"

"They are," Fallon said. "Why didn't I think of it sooner? You can go sleep in them. They're a short walk through the forest. We can take you."

"No, stay here and keep reading," I said. "We'll find them."

"It won't take much time for us to take you," Aislinn said.

"We have little time left." I rubbed my palms together. "Don't you sense it?"

Aislinn's scowl deepened. "I do. I'm trying hard not to though."

"We can't pretend any longer."

"You're right. Go have a nap and we'll keep searching." She turned to the cart of books as though renewed with vigor to research our problems.

Fallon gave us directions to the caravans then Malachi and I walked through the library. There were so many humans inside it was strange to think until a few days ago we'd never met one. They weren't so different from us. Except for our magical powers and soon we might not have those. I longed to cry, but I didn't have the time or the luxury to succumb to my desolate emotions.

My guards fell into step with us, and we told them the plan. They didn't look happy, but they kept to their duty to protect me.

The garden was quiet when we stepped from the underground stairs. Everyone appeared to be in the library. Butterflies hovered from flower to flower and for once the sun was shining. Since we'd been here, the weather was gray and cold. The beams of sunlight put an extra bounce in my pace to get to the caravans. I'd never seen them before either, but I had read about them in human books back home.

Malachi extracted a knitted hat from his pocket and slid it onto my head. My scalp vibrated from the brush of his fingers. "There you go as human as you'll get."

I smiled. "At least you don't have a crown to hide."

He flicked his fingers through his hair. "There are perks to not being royal."

My smile grew. I loved how he wasn't afraid to tease me. My royal status never affected our friendship so these new feelings I was experiencing for him shouldn't affect us.

"Aye, but not as many as there are to being royalty."

"Please," he scoffed. "You realize I have it way better than you."

"Only because you're friends with me." I stopped at the door in the wall.

Ivo walked through first then motioned us forward. We walked through the village, and I couldn't help but watch the humans go about their daily lives. They took little notice of us this time as they all appeared to be busy scurrying between houses and shops. Little children ran past us laughing and giggling. It reminded me of the way Malachi, and I had been so carefree in the Summer Court as children.

"We have to help them too," I said. "We can't let Earth die either."

Malachi gave me his patient smile. "One problem at a time."

"Aye." I stomped off.

He caught up to me and captured my elbow in his warm palm sending those conflicting sensations through my body.

"Stay close," he whispered. "You may appear human, but you're not."

"Neither are you," I whispered back heatedly.

"You're so grumpy when you're tired," he muttered under his breath.

"I heard you."

"Too bad." He let go of my elbow. "The sooner you have a nap the better."

"I'm not a child," I ground out between my teeth.

"Oh, I'm very aware of the fact." His jaw clenched and unclenched as we walked side by side out of the village and across the hillside.

"What's that supposed to mean?"

"Nothing," he snapped.

"Don't tell me nothing. We tell each other everything."

Why were we picking a fight with each other?

He hauled in a deep breath. Once again, my gaze lingered on the muscular form of his chest. I longed to throw myself into his arms and be against his body. Have him hold me tight and tell me I wasn't the only one having lustful thoughts. I was sleep-deprived. Perhaps this was why I couldn't stop looking at Malachi like he was the tastiest blueberry in existence.

"Not everything."

"Wait." I skidded to a stop outside the forest as pain flared in my heart. "You don't tell me everything?"

Now I sensed the tears welling in the backs of my eyes. I believed he was my best friend. The one person I counted on. We had absolute truth between us and now he was telling me we didn't. Why did that hurt me so much?

He flicked his gaze away unable to look me in the eye and lie to me.

"Well," I said, walking off along the track into the forest. "I'm glad I'm aware now."

"Ciara, wait," he called.

"What for?" I hurried my pace. "So, you can lie to me?"

"I've never lied to you?"

"What then?" I spun around walking backward a few steps.

"I don't tell you everything which differs from lying."

"But it's lying by omission."

"I bet there are things you haven't told me."

He placed his hands on his hips and scowled at me.

I flicked my hair over my shoulders and spun back around ignoring his bait. I'd told him everything. All my secrets, my fears, my hopes. Well... apart from these new sensations I was having around him here on Earth and when I wished he was my fated mate... no I was right to keep my feelings to myself. Wishes like mine didn't matter for fate would send us our mates and nothing we said or did would change our destiny.

The forest trees grew thicker. The pathway turned gloomier. Mossier too. My feet slipped on the moss, but Malachi saved me from falling over with his muscular arms. Damn him for always being there. For holding me so tenderly. For the raging desire my body was now experiencing whenever he touched me.

And damn him for not being my fated mate.

It wasn't fair. We were perfect for each other. He kept a hand hovering over my lower back ready to catch me if I fell again. He'd always catch me. I trusted him, but what hadn't he told me? And why wouldn't he tell me? What could be so bad he wouldn't tell me his best friend?

The path ended in a clearing. In the middle of the forest lay a field of wildflowers. Pretty pink, white, and blue flowers dotted the landscape of vibrant green. Standing tall amongst the beautiful nature were stunning caravans painted in bright colors. They stood out amongst the flora, but they also complimented it.

"Which ones can we use?" Emer asked.

"Fallon said any of them."

Emer nodded. "I'll take the first watch while the rest of you sleep."

Ivo stepped forward. "I'll keep watch too," she said. "I slept in the barracks back in the library, so I'll be good until we get back there."

My gaze snapped to Malachi and then away right away. Why had I suddenly thought about sharing a caravan with him? I didn't want to be alone, but we couldn't sleep together. We were only friends. Friends didn't sleep together. Plus, the desire building inside me when we touched would make it hard.

"I'll take the blue one. I think Aislinn said this one is Fallon's."

"Right," Malachi said. "I'll sleep next door then." He turned to the guards. "Wake me if you need to. I'll help protect Ciara."

I rolled my eyes and stomped up the stairs of the blue caravan. As if I needed protection. I was strong. Powerful. I was a Fae royal princess. I opened the door and shut it more forcefully than necessary. Annoyed. Emotional and on the verge of collapse.

So that's what I did. I fell face-first onto the mattress, buried my head in the pillow, tugged the blankets over me, and let go of the tears I'd been battling.

CHAPTER NINE
MALACHI

I REALIZED SHE'D BE crying. I recognized the signs on her face. The way her eyes would glisten even brighter when she fought tears. The way her throat would bob with each swallow. And the way her lips would pout, made me want to kiss her even more than I already did. I wanted her to be happy, not crying. Why had I said I kept things from her? The only thing I kept from her was the love I wanted to give to her as a mate and not a friend. The way I hungered for her body and the sexual things I wanted to do to her. But she didn't feel that way about me. She longed for her fated mate. I wouldn't take her chance at finding him away from her.

It was a stupid thing to say I kept secrets. I only kept one. I blamed the lack of sleep, but was it my tiredness? Or did I want her to learn I loved her? Longed to kiss and touch every inch of her body to see what she liked. Craved to know if she'd moan from an intimate touch to her breasts, between her legs... I couldn't imagine her with anyone but me.

I climbed into the caravan beside hers and closed the door quietly, then I climbed onto the thick mattress of the bed. It was soft. Not as soft as my bed back home, but it was comfortable. I needed sleep. My head was muddled. Being on Earth was making me experience things in another way.

Perhaps not in a different way, but more intense. The constant desire in my body to be as close to Ciara's body as possible. To lay in a bed like this and pleasure her all day and night. The constant throb in my cock to be inside of her.

I'd never imagined telling Ciara I loved her more than as a friend, but being here it was all I thought about besides making love to her. When I wasn't reading the books that was. There was an insistent urge inside me to get the words out. To lay them at her feet and grovel for her to love me back. Maybe if we both found our fated mates here on Earth, then I'd be free from this feeling, but I couldn't imagine loving anyone as much as I loved Ciara.

I rolled over and squeezed my eyes shut. How I longed to go into the same caravan as her. To hold her in my arms and embrace her while she cried those tears she was crying right now. My heart was breaking, not being able to give her what she needed.

But they did not fate her to me.

I should leave her alone.

But I couldn't.

I climbed off the bed and opened the door. Ivo gawked over his shoulder at me and raised an eyebrow in question. I didn't even defend my actions. It was wrong. She was royalty. I wasn't. But she was my best friend before anything else, so I walked over to her caravan.

Raising my fist, I knocked on the door.

"I'm asleep," she exclaimed.

"Funny you can speak in your sleep." I twisted the knob and opened the door.

She picked up a pillow and threw it at my head. "I don't want to see you right now."

"Ciara?" I beseeched. "I'm sorry. The last few days have been hard on both of us. I wanted to check you were all right."

"Now you've seen, you can leave." She sat up and dashed the tears away from her cheeks.

"Shite I made you cry." There went my heart ripping out of my chest and landing at my feet ready for her to stomp on it.

"You did not." She lifted her chin.

"I'm sorry," I said, gripping the knob behind my back to stop myself from racing across the small space and gathering her into my arms. "I should go."

"You indeed should." Her bottom lip wobbled.

"No." I groaned.

I was across the small space in two strides and had her gathered in my arms a heartbeat later. My heart was mine to give, and I would always give it to her. She sobbed and shoved at my chest then another heartbeat later she clung to me and cried. I rubbed her back in soothing strokes letting her get her emotions out. I couldn't imagine how hard it would be to see your father dying when we were immortal. My parents were alive and well but if we didn't fix the spring, then we'd all end up like the King. I couldn't imagine seeing my parents dying or them seeing me die. How difficult it was to realize the fate of all the Fae hinged on us finding a cure for the Spring of Life. Sure, she had me, her brothers and sisters, and her mother too, but when there was this much pressure she was bound to crack at some point in time. We all inevitably did. At least she was safe to do so in my arms.

My hand drifted higher and higher until I was stroking her radiant hair through my fingertips and trailing my palm down her back. Her cries softened as did her breathing. Her limbs loosened from around me and her body grew heavy in my arms. I held her for longer even though she was asleep.

Reluctantly, I eased her out of my arms, laid her head tenderly on the pillow, and climbed off the bed. I tucked the covers around her body wishing I could stay and hold her the entire time she slept but the guards were already questioning my actions and if I stayed with her, then it wouldn't be right. Once again I had to remind myself I wasn't her fated mate. I didn't have the right to hold her in her sleep.

But as her best friend, I still had the right to comfort her when she was upset.

I'd performed my role and now it was time for me to leave as much as I didn't want to, I always wanted the best for her.

I leaned down and kissed her forehead, whispering the words I longed to say, "I love you."

Even though she didn't acknowledge my declaration, my heart lightened for having said it the way I'd always wanted to say it. I left the caravan and almost walked into Emer.

"What were you doing in there?" she asked, crossing her arms over her chest.

"I made sure Ciara got to sleep."

"Mm-hm."

I tried to step around her, but she blocked my path. I crossed my arms matching her stance and raised an eyebrow.

"It's amazing the things you see when you're a bodyguard."

"There was nothing to see." I uncrossed my arms and threw my hands up in the air. My eyebrows rose in surprise at the glowing power in my palms. "She was upset. I apologized. Then I hugged her. That was it."

She tapped her fingers on her arm. "So sweet of you," she drawled. "Above all since you were an ass toward her earlier."

I shoved my hands behind my back. "We're all struggling here."

"Aye. It's a lot to take in knowing the spring is dying, the King too and we'll follow soon." She lowered her arms.

My eyebrows shot up. "I'm surprised they told you."

"There aren't many secrets in the King's guard."

"How long have you known?"

"We've suspected there was a disturbance for a while."

"But you said nothing?"

"No." She shook her head. "We trust the King to keep us safe. And now he can no longer do so in his state we'll trust his children will step up and do their best for our kingdom and our people."

I blew out a breath through my teeth as my hands glowed even brighter. My power wanted an outlet. "No pressure."

She raised her eyebrows. "Is your power unstable? We've heard about this happening to others too."

"Dia." Was there nothing the guards didn't recognize?

I closed my eyes and placed my palms together. I concentrated on the steady beat of my heart. The pulse of my power thrumming through my veins. I slowed my breathing. Centered my thoughts. I wouldn't let my power rule me. The gods made my power for good. I needed the control in check to keep it that way. Inch by inch the unstable sensation of my power receded until I was back in control. I opened my eyes and stared into Emer's concerned face.

"All good."

She cocked her head to the side. "You are strong. You should have been a guard." She slapped me on the shoulder and then laughed. "But then you wouldn't have been able to moon over the princess."

"What?" I spluttered.

"Like I said, being the princess's bodyguard means we see things others don't."

"Such as?"

"You can play dumb all you like, but you understand what I'm talking about. We see the way you look at Ciara with love in your eyes. The way you watch her every movement as though she was the most beautiful woman in any world." She stepped aside.

My breathing shortened. A swirl of nerves circled my stomach. If they saw, then without a doubt others did too, and Ciara. What if she noticed?

"Don't worry, Malachi, your secret is safe with us. Us guards stick together."

"I'm not a guard."

"Could have fooled me with the way you protect Princess Ciara."

I walked past her and down the steps of the caravan. Once my feet hit the cool soil, I was even more grounded. The mere contact soothed my churning emotions and powers. After what Emer said they might have turned volatile.

I turned my head over my shoulder and said, "She's my best friend."

Emer smiled. "One day I want someone to look at me the way you look at Princess Ciara."

CHAPTER TEN
CIARA

I WOKE UP ALONE. Even though Malachi held me while I'd cried myself to sleep, he'd left. I sighed and punched the pillow. What was I expecting? We couldn't sleep in the same bed. That was for fated mates to spend long loving nights together tangled in each other's arms. I scrambled from the bed before my wayward thoughts took me to the place of dreaming. A place where Malachi and I were in this bed as fated mates. Naked and touching.

My body heated to an inferno with one thought, but I didn't feel confused to have these feelings for Malachi. More like it was the right thing for us both. I didn't understand how one night of sleep could change the way I saw things. My feelings for Malachi were clear now. There was no other explanation for it. I was in love with him.

On shaking legs, I walked to the door and flung it open wide letting in the cool breeze of the night. The sun had well and truly set while I was asleep. Ivo and Emer jerked their heads my way, their stances changing in an instant ready to defend me, but it was myself I needed defending from. What if I ruined everything with my feelings for a man who wasn't my fated mate?

"I'm all right," I said and walked down the stairs.

Ivo cocked his eyebrow but turned his head back to investigate the forest.

"Is there something out there?"

"Not that I've seen." He grunted. "The forest is alive at night with animals though."

"Should I be worried?"

"No, they sound like small animals."

"Oh, aye, I read in the books large predators like wolves and bears were driven to extinction after we left Earth," I said.

"A lot has changed."

"I wouldn't know by looking, but aye, from what I've read about this realm there appears to have been changes in the hundreds of years." My finger pressed against my temple. "I suppose change is inevitable, but it makes me wonder if us leaving here caused the humans and the Earth problems."

"Are you sure you've had enough sleep, Princess?" he asked.

"Aye, I'm rested and ready to tackle more books."

He smiled in a way that reminded me of Father, a kind, fatherly smile, so I turned away at once.

"Is Malachi sleeping?"

"He is."

"I guess we'll wait until he wakes then." I slumped down onto the steps and sat on the wooden rungs. The timber was smooth, worn over the many years of the caravan's use.

"You could always wake him," Emer said with a wink.

Why was she winking?

"Oh, no, I couldn't, possibly." I blushed imagining waking Malachi with kisses, and him being excited to see me in the way of fated mates.

When would my infatuation end? It was getting worse each day now. Perhaps when he found the woman who was his fated mate, I'd get over my senseless feelings for my best friend.

"There's food in the caravan over there," Ivo said. "If you're hungry."

"I'm good."

He grunted again.

Silence descended between us. I tipped my head back and stared at the stars of Earth. They twinkled as though blinking at me.

"Did you know most humans believe in one God?"

Another grunt.

"Imagine if they learned the truth there are many Gods."

A door creaked open, and Malachi stepped from the caravan beside mine looking sleep-rumpled and sexy. His hair spiked at odd angles, making my fingers twitch to run through and smooth the strands back into place. His shirt hung from his firm body lopsided thanks to an undone button at the top, and a glorious expanse of his chest was on display. My mouth watered to trail my tongue over his skin. To taste every inch of him.

"We have one God too. Dia," Malachi said.

I squished my lips together. Was I drooling? Heat pooled between my legs and an insistent throb pounded from my core. I longed for Malachi. For us to be together as lovers. Was my body reacting to my desires?

"True." I stood with a start trying to force my thoughts away from wanting to touch him. "I was musing while waiting for you to wake."

"I'm awake. Let's head back." He stepped down the stairs of the caravan.

I jerked to a stand and hurried toward the path back into the woods so Malachi wouldn't touch me and send my desires even higher than they already were. Ivo was already one step in front of me as though she sensed my need to escape into the dense thickness of the evergreen forest. Thank goodness Fallon gave us directions before we left because the forest was difficult to traverse and would be easy to become lost inside the trees.

Malachi caught up with me, his longer legs easily catching my rushed pace. "Did you have a good sleep?"

"I slept well, thank you. I'm refreshed and ready to tackle the problems again."

His fingers brushed mine as we walked sending the tingling sensation through my hand and up my arm. Did he realize what his touch did to me? Or was he simply being his usual friendly self? He inched closer until his entire body was so close that little sparks of arousal shot off through my body.

"I'm glad."

I cleared my throat and willed myself to not think of Malachi as anything other than my best friend. "What about you?"

"I dreamed we found a cure."

"You did!" I swung sideways in my excitement, my hand hitting his thigh and almost stroking across his cock. My cheeks heated so much that my face most likely glowed a bright red.

"It was a dream. I'm not a prophet," he said, seemingly unaffected by my accidental touch.

"No, you're not Saltine, but I'm taking it as a good sign."

Saltine was our old witch seer who used to help us before the Trappers. We'd assumed she'd died since she was a witch and mortal, but Lorcan had seen her not that long ago. Which made me question how she was still alive. And also, if she was more than a witch. Plus, Pepper, Lorcan's mate, was related to Saltine, so I wanted to know because Pepper had survived Lorcan's Fae mating mark when as a mortal witch she shouldn't have. No mortal had ever survived a Fae mating mark.

Plus, Saltine had given Lorcan messages. She had one for Aislinn that had come true. She'd found her fated mate. Then there was the one for Mother telling her it was almost time. Time for what? Did Mother comprehend we were about to die? I shook my head. She wouldn't keep that to herself. So, what was it almost time for Mother to tell us what? I longed to head back to the Summer Court and ask her, but I doubted she'd tell me. Aislinn had said when she asked Mother, she wouldn't tell her.

If Father was stable and not lying unconscious, would she tell him? Surely, she'd tell her fated mate anything?

I peeked sideways at Malachi, I'd told him everything my whole life apart from my new feelings. Yet he'd kept secrets from me. Perhaps we weren't as close as I thought.

With each step deeper into the forest, the animals quietened as they hid from us intruding in their home. We'd never harm an animal though. Malachi raised his hands drawing on his powers. He made a ball of light to illuminate the path so we wouldn't get lost. The ball hovered in front of us shining on the mossy path lighting our way. Shadows danced from the trees beside us across the path. Our footfalls were silent on the spongy soil. It was eerily beautiful in this forest. An owl hooted in the distance. A growl rumbled from the undergrowth.

"A badger," Ivo said. "We're no doubt in his territory."

"Not for long," Malachi said. "The exit is up ahead."

I longed to return to the library. To the books. The sleep while short had rejuvenated me, or maybe it was the cleansing cry or the comforting hug from Malachi. Or the realization I was in love. Perhaps it was all of those things which had relieved me of my fatigue.

We walked out of the forest leaving behind the animals and birds, the coolness under the canopy of the trees, and the quietness. Our steps took us back down the lush green hillside. Malachi dissolved his ball of light long before we arrived at the village. Golden streetlights lit the paths there, and we had no trouble walking the cobblestone streets back to the garden at the end of the village. The wall once again surprised me with how well it blended into the space. I suppose it was the magic of the spring inside or a testament to the Fellowship for creating a safe place for the spring. There was so much to learn here.

"How do we get back in?" Ivo asked.

The door opened, and a member of the Fellowship held up a lantern glowing in the dark of the evening's blackness. "Through the door."

I smothered my laugh at his dry humor. Humans were interesting creatures. I saw why we'd lived with them in harmony for so long before the Trappers. Even saw how Fae might fall in love with humans while knowing they'd never be truly mated or even fated to be together. Happiness transpired even without fate stepping in and making it happen. Should I give up the notion fate would send me and Malachi a fated mate each? Should I ask him to be happy with me? Would he even want me as a lover? Would he be happy to learn I was in love with him?

I shoved my thoughts aside because I needed to focus on our problems with the spring. My love life or lack of it, would have to wait. We walked through the brambles of the garden and down the flight of stairs to the underground library. I paused at the bottom, my mouth fell open, and my eyes couldn't believe the sight before them.

Lorcan and Pepper stood talking with two Fellowship members. My brother and his fated mate turned. My heart almost stopped inside my chest. Why were they here?

"Is Father...?" I asked through the tightness in my throat, not even able to voice the words whirling through my mind.

"He's still sleeping," Lorcan said.

My shoulders sagged. I thought he'd come to tell me Father had died, but then again, wouldn't I have sensed it in the connection with our powers?

"Why are you here then?"

Lorcan frowned. "Nice way to greet your favorite brother."

My lips twitched. "Who said you were my favorite?"

He smirked. "There's no way Rian is your favorite brother."

"And why is that?" I placed my hands on my hips.

"Because I'm the one who snuck your books back from Earth whenever I traveled here."

I rushed across the small distance between us and hugged him.

"I'm glad you're here."

"See, I'm your favorite." He released me and turned to Pepper. "Told you."

Pepper rolled her eyes. "Your ego knows no boundaries."

"You quite like my ego," Lorcan said.

I groaned. "Please stop. It's bad enough with Aislinn and Fallon here, I don't think I can take another pair of recently fated mates."

"What are you saying about me?" Aislinn asked walking down the staircase with Fallon by her side. "I'm your favorite sister."

"None of you are my favorite," I said then huffed.

Malachi chuckled beside me.

"Shh." I touched a finger to his mouth.

His eyes widened as our gazes locked. Heat bounced between us. His lips were soft beneath my skin and the tingle in my fingertip danced up my arm. I dropped my hand as though I'd placed it in a pot of boiling water.

"You're both wrong, I'm her favorite," Roisin said.

I spun and stared at Roisin stepping from behind Lorcan.

"What are *you* doing here? Father would not approve."

Roisin pouted. "I'm here to help Father."

"Go home, Roisin," I said.

"No." She folded her arms around her waist. "I'm here to help and no one can stop me."

I rubbed my forehead. "Dia, help us. When Father wakes and finds out we let you come to Earth..." I shook my head.

"*If* he wakes," Roisin said.

I swallowed the fear her words induced. She was right. There was no when there was only an if. And it wouldn't happen if we didn't get back to the books.

"All right," I said. "The more eyes reading the books the better."

CHAPTER ELEVEN
MALACHI

T HREE DAYS LATER, CIARA sat up straight in the chair beside me. She'd been slumped over lagging from lack of sleep again. Lorcan, Pepper, and Roisin had read many books, Aislinn and Fallon too, not to mention the Fellowship members. We'd consumed pages and pages of endless knowledge. The trouble was there were too many books and not enough time to read them.

Ciara stared at me. Her eyes were wider than I'd ever seen them. The indigo of her eyes shone around the blue. Dia, she was so beautiful. Why couldn't I tell her I loved her? Would it be so bad? Now wasn't the time, but maybe soon...

"I—"

She closed the book and trailed her finger over the title. The Enchantment of Water Sorcery. Wasn't that the book from the magical bookshelf? She closed the book and read the page in the book again, put her finger on the paper, and trailed it across the written words.

"What is it?"

"I'm not one hundred percent sure, but I think I found something."

"Good or bad?"

I wasn't sure I could take another night of her crying herself to sleep. Her happiness meant more than anything to me.

"I'm not sure," she said again. "This book is about Water Sprites, not sorcerers like I thought with the title. It says their magic is all-powerful over water."

"Give me the book." I slid it across the table in front of me.

With each word I read, my eyes bulged, and I bet they appeared the way Ciara's eyes did.

"This might be it." I pointed at a drawing. "These are the same drawings we found in the other book back home of the statues Rian described above the waterfall. The statues are protectors of the Water Sprite kingdom."

"Aye," she lowered her voice. "Did we find the people and the place where to find them who can help us?"

"I'm not sure," I said echoing her words. "From what this book says though it sounds promising."

"What if it's not the right place?"

"But what if it is? What if the Water Sprites are the only people who can fix our spring?"

"Do we tell the others?" she asked.

"We'll have to. We can't disappear without telling them where we're going."

Her eyes glistened as she gazed at me. "What if we get their hopes up and we're wrong?"

I clasped her shoulder. "That won't be our fault if that happens."

"It will be." She sucked in a breath, her chest expanding and making my gaze dip to her breasts for many seconds before I remembered what Ivo said and snapped my gaze back toward her eyes. I'd been so careful the last few days to keep thinking of Ciara as my best friend and not the woman I was in love with.

It'd been hard, but I think I'd pulled it off. I didn't want her brother and sisters to learn of my true feelings for Ciara. They'd tell me she deserved her fated mate, and I understood that. It was why I'd never told her I loved her.

"It won't," I said with conviction.

"We should go now. The sooner the better to see if the book is right and that those statues lead to the Water Sprite kingdom."

"Agreed." I stood and picked up the book. "Let's show them."

"If Rian and Sophia were here, they'd confirm if those sketches were what they saw at the top of the waterfall and the ones that shot the deadly darts stopping them from exploring further. Then they'd have hope we found the answer to getting past the darts and the secrets inside."

"At least the book tells us how to get past the darts." I placed the book back on the desk in front of Ciara. "Stay here. I'll get everyone to come to you."

Ciara's once hopeful face had fallen in the space of a minute. Time was so different here on Earth, but I'd become accustomed to the way the humans peered at the clock on the wall and did certain things according to the time. They served meals three times a day. The Fellowship had surprised me with how well they'd accepted us into their fold. They'd fed us. Offered us a place to sleep and wash up. They'd even provided us with human clothes to wear to fit in with the village, not that we'd ventured out apart from our one trip to the caravans to sleep.

I walked down the aisles of bookshelves and found Aislinn and Roisin deep in conversation. Roisin didn't appear happy, and neither did Aislinn. I cleared my throat because I didn't want to interrupt whatever discussion was happening between the two sisters.

Aislinn turned my way, her fingers sliding over the hilt of a dagger strapped around her waist. I'd been on the receiving end of those flying daggers more than once over the years, but they'd never hit me. Aislinn always made sure she threw them close enough to scare me but not to hurt me. Ciara always laughed when she did it and teased me about my face as the daggers flew past me. Squeezing my lips together, I refrained from smiling at the way it made Ciara happy to tease me. I'd take all of Aislinn's daggers to hear her laugh.

"What is it?" Aislinn asked.

"Ciara found something."

"I knew she would," Roisin said and brushed past me.

Her youthful exuberance was infectious. Aislinn followed her at a quick pace. I left them to wait with Ciara and searched the many aisles looking for Lorcan too. I found Lorcan standing with Pepper by the magical bookcase.

Pepper's cloak flared as she spun around to face me. "Damn, you snuck up on us."

Lorcan turned. "It's usually Ciara doing the sneaking. Where is she?"

"Back at the table." I nodded my head toward the entrance where Ciara hadn't ventured far from after her initial panic attack. As much as she longed to come to study the magical bookshelf, her phobia wouldn't allow her to come back here again. "Did you find anything here?"

"There is powerful magic at play," Pepper said, skimming her hands through the air in front of the bookshelf. "I can't make it out though."

"We'll figure it out," Lorcan said.

"It's interesting how much magic is here in this one place." I rubbed my chin. "Ciara needs to see you all. She may have found an answer to our problems."

"Why didn't you say so sooner?" Lorcan asked as he too brushed past me.

Pepper patted my hand. "Don't mind him, he hasn't been himself these days."

"I understand what you mean. Ciara is out of sorts too. So am I if I'm being honest."

"The gods tied your powers to the spring, it's understandable now the spring is unstable your powers will be too."

We fell into step back down the long library.

"For all I've read over the years, I still don't understand everything."

She cackled. "No one ever will."

"Great," I grumbled.

"No one should understand everything. It would make them dangerous."

I tilted my head to the side to study the profile of the witch. "In what way?"

"Knowledge makes people powerful. Power makes people dangerous. Look at what the Trappers did. They believed they'd take Fae's powers from them which made them dangerous to the Fae."

"We have power though and we're not dangerous."

"Aren't you?" She raised her eyebrows. "You might be the most dangerous for not using your powers for good."

"So, you're saying no matter what power is dangerous."

"I suppose." She pinched the skin between her eyes. "I'm so tired perhaps I'm not making sense."

"We're all tired."

She yawned. "I have sleep potions that will help."

"No time for sleep."

We arrived at the table where Ciara sat, her palms splayed across the pages of the open book before her as though she was stopping her sisters and brother from reading it. Fallon had his arm around Aislinn's waist as though holding her back. He must have learned Ciara had found something and came here too because I hadn't found him to tell him. They were all excited and going by the expressions on their faces, nervous too.

I believed in Ciara. If she thought this was the answer to our problems, then she was right. She needed to believe in herself. I'd be by her side every step of the way for her to figure it out. I couldn't imagine a life where she wasn't in it.

CHAPTER TWELVE
CIARA

"CALM DOWN EVERYONE," I said channeling Mother for her calmness when dealing with her children. How she ever managed all seven of us I'd never comprehend. We were all different yet similar.

"We're all here now so tell us what you found," Aislinn said.

I thrust back the chair little by little and stood. "It might be nothing, but it might be something."

"Stop dragging it out," Lorcan said.

"I'm not. I don't want you all to get your hopes up and it is for nothing."

"Ciara, hope is all we have left," he said.

"Aye." I nodded. He was right. If we didn't have hope, then what did we have left? Nothing. We'd be nothing but a piece of history soon. Even then we wouldn't be history to any humans but the Fellowship. Other humans didn't believe we existed anymore.

Lifting the book, I drew in a grounding breath, sensing my power pulsing in my palms, I pointed at the picture in the book. "This fits the description of the statues Rian and Sophia found at the top of the waterfall."

Lorcan drew the book from under my hand and peered closer at the sketches. "I'd say you're right. We should ask Rian and Sophia to confirm."

I shook my head. "It'll take too long. Malachi and I are going to the waterfall now."

"Too long?" Lorcan cocked his eyebrow. "It doesn't take us long at all to travel through the Veil."

"Our powers are unstable, traveling might go wrong."

"But you're willing to risk yourself to travel through the Veil to the waterfall and check this out without knowing for certain?"

"I can't sit here and read any more books. This is the biggest clue we've found. Besides, those statues refer to the Water Sprites. Beings with powerful water magic. Doesn't that seem important?"

"Water Sprites?" Aislinn shrugged out of Fallon's arms and threw one of her knives across the room. It landed on the wooden side of the shelf. "Why would they harm us?"

"I'm not saying they did." I sighed. This was going as well as I thought it would. "We won't learn anything until Malachi, and I go there and talk to them."

"We should all go," Roisin said.

"No. I need you all to stay here and keep researching because if I'm wrong, then we still don't understand how to cure the spring."

"You think the Water Sprites can cure our Spring of Life?" Roisin asked.

"From the small amount of information in the book, then aye, I think they would be able to with their powers."

Roisin smiled. "You truly have found what we're looking for."

"Please don't say that." My bottom lip quivered.

Roisin stepped forward and hugged me. "I believe in you. We all do."

"She's right," Malachi said. "We all believe you're the smartest."

"Hey," Lorcan said. "I'm the smartest."

I spluttered out a laugh. Trust my brother to lighten the mood. I squeezed Roisin back. My little sister was my biggest champion, but she didn't comprehend how dark my powers and thoughts might go.

I poked Lorcan in the chest. "When I get back, we'll have to settle this once and for all."

"What do you suggest?" He puffed out his chest ramming it into my finger.

Pepper cackled. "You're so old yet so immature."

He caught her around the waist, swung his mate up into his arms, and kissed her into silence.

I glanced away but my gaze landed on Malachi. Heat bounced around the room with the way Pepper and Lorcan were displaying their fated mate status. I'd never been jealous of my siblings but right now I wanted what they had. Happiness with their fated mate even when life was uncertain.

"Dia, go find a spare room," Aislinn grumbled.

"Like you and Fallon do?" Lorcan asked after ending the steamy kiss.

Fallon laughed. Aislinn lifted a dagger. Roisin smiled and then skipped off into the depths of the library. My family might be crazier than most, but they were mine, and I loved them very much.

"All right, time to tell my guards where we're heading."

Emer appeared from nowhere. "No need, we heard everything. We'll go with you to the waterfall and protect you from the danger."

I grimaced. From what Rian had said about the statues, they'd shot poisonous darts from their faces. The book said the poison was toxic, but it also said announcing your presence to the faced statues will go one of two ways. Darts shot at you or an entrance into the Water Sprites kingdom opened.

We had a fifty-fifty chance of it going either way.

Ivo and Emer walked with Malachi and me back to the secluded setting of the caravans. We'd agreed it was the best place for me to open the Veil. With how unstable our powers were, if anything bad happened, then the damage wouldn't hurt the Fellowship or the humans in the village. After working by their side, I didn't want to hurt any of them. They'd become our friends. Our allies. We needed to protect them. They'd protected our existence for years.

A nervous energy bounced between us on the path back through the forest. Malachi shoved his hands into the pockets of his human clothes. I still wore a dress. Made from thick human material I didn't like, they said it made me fit in better. The knitted hat on my head matched the dress. I suppose if I was human the material would keep me warm in this cool weather of Ireland.

I couldn't wait to visit Crystal Creek where Briana found her fated mate Sledge, the Alpha wolf shifter, and Saoirse had met her fated mate, Arrow, another wolf shifter in the same pack. Saoirse had been in heat at the time and had fallen pregnant. It was a miracle she'd given birth and not lost the baby as most Fae did these days. Excitement to see the place my sisters lived happily with their fated mates warred with my nervousness. What would Malachi think of my sister's fated mates? He'd yet to meet them or my nephew. If we were to have a child together, what would it be like?

I forced a finger between my eyes. Why was I thinking about Malachi again? About us having a baby.

"Are you all right?" Malachi asked.

"Aye." I dropped my hand and watched as small shadows engulfed my fingertips. I drew my power back before it swallowed me whole.

Malachi frowned but said nothing else.

Shadows were everywhere but not from my power. The twisted trees in the forest seemed to come alive as the wind swirled around us. Sound traveled with the breeze. I could have sworn I heard a woman speak. I paused and spun around searching for the source of the distorted words.

"What is it?" Emer asked scanning the trees for any threat.

"Didn't you hear it?"

"Hear what?"

I cocked my head and listened to the wind rustling through the leaves. No other words came. I must have imagined it.

"Never mind."

I walked along the moss-covered path again. The ground was slippery under my feet, but I placed each foot carefully one after another until we left the eerie forest and stepped into the clearing. Here the grass was soft under my toes and tickled between them. Dainty flowers bloomed amongst the foliage. If I pretended hard enough, I could be back in the Summer Court before any of this happened. The area was that pretty, it could be a part of our magical kingdom.

I stopped in the center of the caravans and lifted my hands. As I called on my power, I manipulated the Veil the way Saoirse and Lorcan had taught me. Magic pulsed and tore at me. My power surged sending dark shadows up my arms. I thrust the power forward into the Veil, but nothing happened. The lock held.

"No," I cried, urging more and more power into the Veil. I may not have been as well practiced as my brothers and sisters with unlocking the Veil, but I understood what I needed to do. My arms shook with the force of magic coming from me. Shadows drifted higher toward my neck threatening to suffocate me, but they'd never hurt me simply consume me. Make me dark. Invisible.

Malachi's hands landed on my shoulders, a familiar, comforting embrace. A bright light flared from his palms sending the shadows back down my arms and forcing the power into the Veil. The lock twisted. Popped open. The Veil swirled into existence a shimmering cacophony of dark and light mixed in a beautiful display that made me gasp.

"Faster," I said. "We need to hurry."

Ivo and Emer rushed into the glowing curtain. Malachi kept his connection on me and together we stepped into the Veil. As the curtain closed behind us, the power inside me eased or perhaps it was Malachi's grounding touch that soothed my power. I didn't worry about anything else now he was by my side. I kept my concentration on the place we needed to go. Kept my mind open and the pictures in my head focused on my sister Briana, on Saoirse, and the place she now called home. What seemed like hours later, we stepped from the Veil.

Around us was a different forest. One of red-brown soil, silvery-gray tree trunks, and dull green leaves. A strange animal hopped by on two long back legs. From what I'd read about this place, Australia, the animal was a kangaroo.

"I think we're in the right place."

In the distance, a wolf howled. I pointed in that direction.

"We'll head this way."

"Wolves aren't always pleasant, Princess," Ivo said.

"This one is." I smiled. "It's one of my sister's mates."

"How do you recognize him?"

"Because I'm believing in myself."

Malachi smiled down at me. It was all because of him we were here now. Without his unwavering support and calmness then I wouldn't have been able to open the Veil. We would never have made it to Crystal Creek. My best friend was always there for me.

Now we were one step closer to finding the Water Sprites and asking them to cure our Spring of Life.

CHAPTER THIRTEEN

CIARA

B EFORE WE'D WALKED TOO far through the strangely
scented forest, a big black wolf with striking blue
eyes found us. My guards were alert and on guard but
then the wolf shifted, and Sledge stood in front of us.
Naked.

I lifted my gaze skyward. I so didn't want to see
Briana's fated mate naked. If fate mated me to a shifter,
I don't think I'd handle the jealousy of knowing others
would see him naked.

Sledge laughed. "You Fae can be such prudes
sometimes."

"No offense, Sledge," I said. "But I don't want to be on
the end of Briana's staff."

"She packs a mean hit."

"I'll change back, and you can follow me into town."

"We need to go to the waterfall. Can you take us
there?"

"I should take you to Briana first."

"Ciara found who is hiding up the top of your waterfall," Malachi said.

"Yeah? Who?"

"Water Sprites," I said.

"Huh? I've never heard of them."

"I'm surprised." I dropped my gaze and then stared back up at the pale blue sky. The sun shone through the sparse branches of the forest. It was warm here. Almost like home.

"What do Water Sprites do?" Sledge asked.

"They manipulate water."

"Well, obviously," he drawled. "I'm guessing you think they can fix your spring?"

"Aye," I said.

"I should tell Briana then."

"Of course, after we make it up there."

"Shit," Sledge grumbled. "She'll kick my ass for taking you there and not telling her."

Malachi laughed. I shot him a look to shut him up.

"I'm not asking you not to tell her, but to take us there first before telling her because I don't want to get her hopes up."

"Not this again," Malachi said.

I placed my hands on my hips and faced him. "Are we having this conversation again?"

Malachi sighed and shook his head.

"So, Sledge, are you taking us to the waterfall or are we stumbling around this forest to find it ourselves?"

"I'll take you," he growled. "But remember what Rian said was up there."

"Aye. We found it mentioned in a book. We comprehend how to get by the darts."

Well, I hoped the way worked. Otherwise, the darts might hit us. And the poison. Malachi frowned. He'd read the book too, so he comprehended our chances were fifty-fifty of being shot at. If we were, then I hoped we were as fast as Sophia and Rain at getting out of the way, but I doubted I had the skills of a jaguar shifter.

Sledge shifted back to his wolf form and howled. My skin prickled as my hair stood on end. In such a short amount of time, I'd left the safety of the Summer Court for the relative safety of Ireland and the underground library and now we were out in the open in Australia, surrounded by extended family, but knowing we were about to enter the lair of other powerful beings.

I wasn't sure how they'd take our request either. Were Water Sprites kind creatures? Would they help us?

We walked through the forest, passing by a crystal-clear lake that glowed a shiny blue under the cloudless sky. This place was beautiful. I saw why Saoirse and Briana had made it their new home with their fated mates. At least they both had each other when they lived in the same town. I was almost jealous they'd spend so much time together even after finding their fated mates.

I wasn't sure where I'd end up when I found my fated mate. If I ever found him. Above all if we didn't fix the spring, then I might never find him. Perhaps that would be the best with my feelings for Malachi.

The forest trees thickened into dense bush, but Sledge passed through it with ease in his wolf form. We ducked and weaved through the low-hanging branches brushing more of the eucalyptus scent onto our human clothes. The knitted hat on my head caught on a branch and ripped off.

"Leave it," Malachi said. "There are no humans here to question the flowers in your hair."

I was glad he said that because I didn't like wearing the hat. My head throbbed under the material and now it was free a shiver danced over my scalp as my hair lifted in the gentle breeze. Some branches caught my hair, and it was as though nature was greeting me with a gentle caress.

On and on we walked until Sledge stopped beside a thick wall of vegetation. He pointed his snout at a small entrance at the bottom of the bushes. My anxiety spiked at the sight of the dark entrance. Sledge disappeared through the leaves.

"I'll go first," Ivo said.

We watched him crouch and shuffle through the entrance into who knew where, but if I didn't let my panic take over and I kept the knowledge of this place Rian, Saoirse, and Briana had told us about, then everything would be good because I understood there was a waterfall through those bushes. Even though I couldn't hear it from this side as powerful magic protected this place. It made sense now knowing the entrance to the Water Sprite kingdom was in there that they would protect the only way in with magic.

Malachi crawled through next. If he did this, then so would I. I followed him, holding my breath the entire way through the dark bushes until I made it out to the other side and stood before the glorious waterfall. Water droplets sparkled in the sunbeams streaming into the enclosed area. The water was so clear the pond below glistened like a mirror. Emer followed and then we were all inside the thick wall of bushes that hid this magical place. Sledge shifted again, but he walked to a small backpack on the ground and tugged on shorts.

"You need to head behind the waterfall and climb up. There's a switch or something up there that'll open the entrance to the tunnel," Sledge said.

"A tunnel?" I gulped.

"Through the tunnel is where Rian and Sophia found the statues. They didn't go any further."

"Right." I nodded. "We can do this."

Malachi gave me an encouraging smile even though the skin around his eyes creased with his concerned look. One I'd seen many times over our years together.

"Agreed," Malachi said.

"I'd stay and help, but I'm heading home to tell Briana." Sledge grimaced. "Good luck and don't get yourselves killed."

"Thank you for your help," I said. "Tell Briana to take it easy on you."

Sledge laughed. "As if she'd listen."

"True." I smiled.

Knowing my oldest sister, she wouldn't be easy on her mate, but then I suspected he enjoyed her attitude because they were fated for each other. A perfect match. He stripped the shorts and shifted back into the glorious black wolf before running back out the way we'd come in through the bushes, the tip of his tail the last thing to disappear.

I turned to the waterfall and stared up at the great height of the falling water over the rock face.

"How are we getting up there?" Malachi asked.

"Magic," I said.

CHAPTER FOURTEEN
MALACHI

B EFORE I KNEW IT, Ciara called on her powers and smothered herself in the shadows. She vanished in an instant blending into the rock wall.

"Where did she go?" Emer asked, whipping her head side to side.

I stifled a laugh but then Ciara's shadows engulfed me. Her power tickled my skin. It was a sensation I'd experienced before otherwise I wouldn't have realized her guards couldn't see me either. I loved the way her power caressed my flesh. I always imagined her fingers stroking me the same way her power swirled over my skin.

"Shite, where did Malachi go too?" Ivo asked.

"Princess, this isn't funny," Emer said.

Under normal circumstances, I'd think this was funny. Ciara grabbed my hand and tugged me toward the waterfall. I leaned closer to her since I saw her clearly while engulfed in her shadow magic. It was a game we'd played many times hiding from her brothers and sisters while sneaking around the palace. The things we'd learned while doing it had opened our eyes.

"What are you doing?" I whispered into her ear.

"Shh." She touched a finger to my lips. "They'll hear you. We should go by ourselves."

I shook my head. This was a bad idea. Terrible. But I kept my hand in hers and let her lead me to the edge of the waterfall because I'd follow her anywhere. We inched along the rock wall instead of swimming through the water as Sledge had instructed so they wouldn't see our bodies rippling the water. The rocks were slippery with moisture, and we almost fell twice but Ciara's power snapped toward the wall and anchored us as though a pair of ropes were holding us in place. Each step carried us closer to the water rushing over the cliff face. The force sent a spray of water over us turning our human clothes damp and sticking the material to my skin.

We stopped once we were behind the wall of water. Ivo and Emer's images were blurry through the curtain of water. I eased my grip to release her hand, but she held tight to me.

"Don't let go," she said. "They'll see you."

"Ciara, this is a terrible idea. We need your guards to protect you."

"We have a better chance of being accepted into the Water Sprite kingdom without them. You understand this because you read the same book as me. The book clearly said anyone who enters with weapons will be treated as an enemy and disposed of. The guards won't leave their weapons behind and if they do, they've trained their powers as weapons too. I can't risk their lives. I can't risk this last hope that water magic will fix our spring."

My lips firmed. I didn't disagree with her. What was the point when she was right?

"You should have at least told them."

"They would never have let me go by myself."

I sighed. She was right again. The King's guard took their role seriously.

"I hope I don't regret this." I squeezed her hand. "How are we getting up?"

Ciara smiled and sent a surge of her dark power upward. Thick black shadows shot up the wall.

"And here I thought you were magicking us up there?"

She giggled and then slammed her free hand over her mouth. My gaze landed on her face, drinking in the happy gleam in her eyes. Dia, it made me want to kiss her. I longed to soak her happiness into my body. To make her even happier too by showing her how much my body hungered for hers.

Her gaze met mine and a tangible thread of heat bounced between us. She dropped her hand from her mouth. Ciara's pink tongue darted out along her lips so fast I almost missed it, but I'd fantasized about twining my tongue with her in a lover's kiss for so many years. It would be so easy to sneak kisses while engulfed in her shadows. The things I wanted to do to her, and she didn't have a clue how I felt. Now wasn't the time to tell her either.

She shifted closer to me as though drawn by my thoughts of kissing her lips parted in invitation. I lowered my head. The heat coming from both our bodies was tangible. We were so close her tiny puffs of breath brushed over my lips. It was almost like a kiss itself.

What was I doing?

I dragged my gaze away and stepped into the shadows climbing the wall. We had a job to do. I couldn't keep fantasizing about my best friend. Ciara kept in contact with my skin as though she didn't sense my lustful thoughts to kiss her and devour her body. The contact sent my desire even higher as she threaded her arm through mine linking us at the elbows. She placed one hand on the wall and then tugged her other hand. I lifted my gaze to the great height we'd need to climb. Climbing while connected would be hard, but I trusted her power to keep us safe. I swung toward the wall and together we climbed inch by inch. Her shadows clung to us and the wall like thick cords of rope helping us up the wall. I didn't doubt for a second if I fell, she'd catch me or make a mattress from shadows for me to land on.

My powers throbbed under my skin longing to get free too. When we were younger, we'd played a lot with our powers testing them out on each other and now it was as though if one of us used our powers the other's power responded in tune. Dark and light. As though the two needed each other to be happy. I sure needed Ciara.

"Sophia and Rian said there was a glowing red light hiding a lever," Ciara said.

"I see it up there. We need to go higher."

Ciara's darkness thickened as her power pulsed harder, forcing us up the wall in a hurry, her shadow ropes tugging us higher and higher. We arrived at the glowing spot, and I shoved my hand into it sensing a frigid chill on my skin that didn't bother me at all since I was Fae, but I assumed it was a deterrent to other people. Beside us, a circular rock rolled to the side revealing an entrance to a dark cave.

Shite. This wasn't good. Ciara was afraid of caves, but determination etched the firm set of her mouth.

"Your time to shine." She shot me a smile.

"I'd light up the world for you if you need it." I released the hold on my power and let it engulf my palms.

In the blink of an eye, the entire cave glowed a vibrant white light so radiantly we'd see every nook and cranny on the rock face.

"They said there were no booby traps in here."

"Want to race to the end?" I asked, knowing even though the cave was alight with my powers Ciara would still get the impression of being enclosed. She might even have had a panic attack. The sooner I got us through the cave the better.

"We're too old for races."

"We're never too—"

Ciara raced into the cave before I finished my sentence. Her quick turn of speed sent me racing after her. She peered over her shoulder as I neared her, but then flung her head back around sending her pretty silvery blonde hair shimmering in the light as though they were fine threads. And they were. I longed to run my fingers through them. To hold them as she took my throbbing cock into her mouth. My breath surged in a sharp rush as I forced the desire back down. What was wrong with me feeling this way now while we were on a lethal mission? Perhaps it was the prospect we might not survive if the poisonous darts on the other side of this cave hit us.

I caught up to Ciara and ran by her side altering my stride length, so we kept in line and burst through the other side of the cave together.

"Stop," Ciara said.

I ground to a stop a few steps in front of her since she'd stopped before me. I'd been too caught up in my wayward thoughts to realize she'd stopped.

Before us stood great Redwood trees in the open space atop the rocks. A clearing of grass spread in an inviting blanket to lay upon before the green moss-covered trunks. Sunlight streamed through the outer edges of the trees and bathed us in a delicate glow. The beams hit my skin in a caress reminding me of the Summer Court. There was powerful magic here as there was in the Fae Kingdom making me wonder if we'd shifted into another dimension or if we were still on Earth.

"Now what?" I asked.

"Now we announce our presence and wait for an escort into the Water Sprite kingdom."

I raised my eyebrows. "That easy?"

She lifted her shoulders in a halfhearted shrug and said, "I Princess Ciara O'Cleirigh of the Summer Court and Malachi Byrne request a presence with the Water Sprite Master."

Her voice rang out through the quiet of the forest as though every fiber of the area absorbed her words. After her announcement, a flock of birds flew from the trees and into the sky.

"Now what do we do?"

"We wait," she said, searching beside the cave for a place to rest.

We both spotted the fallen tree at the same time and walked toward it. I dusted off the bark and then waved my hand at the log.

"Your chair, Your Highness."

She dipped a curtsy. "Thank you, kind sir."

We both laughed and sat on the log. The remembered childhood games were the perfect tension release for our wait. Ciara tugged on the material of her damp dress. I was as uncomfortable as her in these damp clothes.

"Humans need better material," she said.

"I agree." I rubbed the shirt clinging to my chest.

Ciara's gaze followed the motion for a moment longer than a simple observation, but she flicked her gaze away before I deciphered if I'd read too much into her stare. Was it dreaming on my part? Was I projecting my desire onto her?

We waited a long time on the log. Neither of us said anything else. We both understood the enormity of the situation. If we didn't talk to the Water Sprites and find out if they would fix our Spring of Life, then we might lose everything soon. So, we'd sit forever, even if forever wasn't that long.

As the sun lowered in the sky, a gray fog rolled through the forest wrapping around the tree trunks in the way Ciara's shadows engulfed whatever she wanted.

A dark shadow stepped toward us through the fog. Ciara stood in a rush and so did I. Another shadow appeared. Then another. Soon half a dozen shadows were walking toward us.

I regretted not bringing her guards with us.

CHAPTER FIFTEEN
CIARA

MALACHI'S HANDS GLOWED WITH an iridescent light that made my power respond. The magical creatures walking toward us stopped in their tracks. The fog swirled thicker coating their presence in a preternatural gray mist. I imagined this was how I appeared when I used my powers.

"Relax, Malachi," I said softly and placed a hand on his arm. "We have to show them we mean no harm."

"I can't even see them," Malachi said. "Who can hide their presence like they did?"

"Me."

His shoulders dropped, and the light disappeared from his hands.

"We mean no harm," I called out to the people in the thick fog.

"Tell your boyfriend that," a husky woman's voice called from the fog.

"He's not my boyfriend," I called back.

The woman appeared through the fog. A shimmering gray dress clung along her curvaceous figure leaving nothing covered since the material was see-through.

"Well then, this changes things," the woman purred stepping closer, bringing the mist with her. "He's very handsome. Malachi, wasn't it?"

"Aye," Malachi said. "And who might you be?"

"Nerita at your service. Any service you require."

"Um." Malachi tugged at the human clothes which were still damp, and his white shirt was see-through too.

I had to keep averting my eyes while we waited because seeing the outline of his muscles through his shirt had made an insistent throb start between my legs. I'd sat on the log for hours upon hours afraid to reposition. Afraid Malachi would be horrified if he comprehended I wanted him as more than a friend.

"These are Kishi, Thames, and Mako."

"I thought there were more of you?" I asked glancing into the fog which still hung heavy in the air.

Nerita flung her thick, long hair over her shoulder. Did it have a sparkle of blue on the strands?

"There were, but it's only us out in the forest now. State your business or be on your way. Although Malachi is welcome to stay." She closed the distance between them and ran a finger over the button at his throat.

Malachi clenched his jaw but said nothing. Why wasn't he swatting her away? Dia, I longed to rip her nail from her finger because she was touching Malachi. I shook my head to clear my thoughts of jealousy. We needed these people.

"I request an audience with your Master."

Her striking blue eyes slid my way. "What for?" she snapped.

"It is a very personal matter and only one I'm willing to discuss with your leader."

"Hmm." She tapped her pointed fingernail on her lip. "Bye-bye." She waved her hand toward the tunnel.

"Please." Malachi's hand shot out and landed on her hip. "Help us."

I'd never seen him touch a woman so intimately before. Sure, it was only her hip, but the way he held onto it suggested otherwise. And the look on his face as he pleaded with her... Envy pounded inside my skull. Had Malachi found his fated mate with this woman? Is that why he was letting her touch him? The reason he was touching her too?

Nerita smiled in a way I didn't like at all. "Sweetheart, since you asked so nicely. Come with us."

She turned toward the forest, but the gray fog hung heavy around the trees making it hard to see where we were walking. I reached my hand out for Malachi out of habit, but he was behind me walking with Nerita. She'd linked her arm through his in the same way I had to climb the wall. The jealousy intensified, but I shoved it down so I could concentrate on where we were walking. The man she'd referred to as Thames walked a pace in front of me, and Mako to the side of me but he didn't touch me thankfully. Kishi walked behind us all, her very blue hair matching her eyes and making it obvious she wasn't a human. I assumed they were all water sprites going by the way their hair glinted blue in varying hues. I had read a little about them in my research, but I hadn't been looking for information on them. Perhaps I should have.

The fog was thick and damp against my skin and clothes. The dreadful material had almost dried while we'd waited, but now they were once again wet, clingy, and itching my skin. Each uncomfortable step through the forest made me want to rip them from my body. Instead, I lifted my chin and marched through the tall trees and fernery of the forest like the princess I was. Fronds brushed against my arms as though testing who I was before accepting I wasn't an enemy and letting me pass.

From inside the fog, two white stone pillars appeared. The carved faces peered down on me judging me even more. My muscles tightened, and I called my power to hover at the ready for this was where the darts nearly hit Rian and Sophia.

A loud gong rang through the forest. The fog muffled the sound, but it rippled on and on as though cocooned inside the magic of this place. I assumed it meant someone had announced our arrival.

Power flared between the two columns in a parting curtain of luminous blue. The eyes on the statues closed. Did this mean it was safe to pass through without the poisonous darts?

Thames strode ahead as though he didn't have a care in the world, so I assumed it meant we were safe to walk through the pillars too. Either that or we were about to die. My foot hovered a split second before I placed it down. Either way, we'd be dead soon if we didn't fix the spring. When nothing shot at us, I let out a small sigh of relief. Thames glanced over his shoulder and sent me a seductive smile. I frowned but kept my irritation in check.

The fog seemed to follow us through the forest and out to the other side. Many buildings were hovering on stilts above a massive expanse of water. My mind whirled at the village laying before us. Thicker fog formed instantly around us until we could no longer see the village. I'd read once the temperature was cold enough on Earth, the vapor condensed into tiny water droplets. And it wasn't cold here. The fog grew and receded too quickly to be anything other than made by magic. If the Water Sprites influenced tiny particles, then they must have enough power to fix our spring, unlike Saoirse who'd had no luck using her powers over water. Perhaps because she wasn't a king and only kings were powerful enough to mend what was broken. But then Father had failed. His powers had helped for a time, but perhaps a being who was the Master of Water magic would be powerful enough to cure our ailments. I had to believe there was someone with more power who could fix our spring.

At long last I'd found my hope.

Turning, I smiled at Malachi over my shoulder, but his gaze was on Nerita who was unabashedly batting her eyelashes at him and chatting happily with him. Malachi seemed interested in whatever she was saying although I couldn't hear her, I saw the way he was leaning in toward her body. Their arms brushed on purpose with each step. I swung back around before I caused her bodily harm.

The fog parted, and a house appeared in front of us. It had a thick thatched roof, but it was the fact the house was on stilts and surrounded by water that surprised me the most. I hadn't noticed we were walking along a boardwalk once we'd entered the village since the fog had covered the fact. One step wrong and I'd have plummeted off the side of the walkway into the water below.

Thames knocked on the door and then opened it.

"Sir Axis Foxlace will see you and only you."

"But?"

"His Kingdom. His rules." Thames shrugged. "Do you still wish to speak with him?"

I turned to Malachi, who at last stared at me. He nodded his head for me to go inside which made my gut twist. Had he found his fated mate? Did he want me to leave them alone so they'd connect? There was no other explanation because Malachi had always been by my side and now, he was telling me to go on without him.

"Aye."

He turned to Nerita as though eager to follow the beautiful water sprite anywhere.

I turned back around and stepped through the door.

CHAPTER SIXTEEN
CIARA

HAULING IN A CENTERING breath, I stepped into the house. The door closed behind me, and I jumped involuntarily. Golden light shone through the ceiling of glass through the misty haze of the fog and lit the welcoming interior in an ethereal light. Plants grew in deep greens throughout the room and made the atmosphere more at ease as though it catered to the elemental magic inside me. Two circular chairs were the focal point of the room and the only furniture apart from the plants.

Footsteps echoed down the stairs, and I lifted my gaze to the man walking down the timber slats who seemed to float in midair. His chest was bare, and his bronzed skin was a tantalizing sight. My gaze followed the lines of his body as though hypnotized by the tight black leather pants hugging his hips and not covering the bulge in his pants at all. My cheeks heated, and I lifted my chin, determined to meet with the Water Sprite Master. To ask for his help. His looks didn't matter.

Not at all.

"Ah," he said, stepping off the last slat and gliding across the room. "You're even more lovely than your mother."

I cocked my head to the side. "You've met my mother?"

"Yes, your father too." He swept his arm toward the chairs. "Shall we sit?"

"As you wish, this is your house and kingdom." I kept my chin high and perched on the edge of a chair.

"I see your parents' ingrained manners in you." He sat on the other circular chair opposite me and spread his thick thighs.

With a substantial force of will I stopped my gaze from dropping to his masculine display.

"How are your parents?"

"I'm not here for idle chit-chat." I tugged on the skirts of my damp dress.

"I imagine not." He placed his hands on his knees and curled his fingers into fists.

"So, you realize what is happening?"

He stood so fast that I had no time to adjust my line of sight, and I faced the bulge between his legs.

"This will not do," he tutted. "Where are my manners? You're uncomfortable in those clothes. Please allow me to show you to a room and I'll have more suitable attire fetched to you."

I jumped to my feet. "I don't need a room or another dress."

His hand snapped out and touched the material on the sleeve of my dress. "Human material is horrendous. A princess should not be wearing it. I won't stand for it. And I won't talk to you while you're wearing those clothes."

"You're being unreasonable," I said.

He narrowed his eyes and leaned closer. "I am not, and you will treat me with respect while you're in my kingdom."

The air crackled with his power. It rolled over every inch of my skin making me even more aware he was a man, and I was a woman. At any other time, I would have stuck to my opinion, but I needed to ask him for help. And by the way, his power buzzed, he had enough to make my request happen.

"I'm sorry," I whispered.

"That's more like it." He smiled with his shiny white teeth showing all predator like he was about to devour his prey and happy about the upcoming meal. "Come with me."

He walked up the stairs, and I hurried to follow him. I didn't want to anger him in his kingdom, but I should have brought my guards with me. What was I thinking leaving them behind?

Each step up the floating slats made it seem like I was walking into the sky. The glass ceiling grew closer until the sight of the sky became clearer. The fog had lightened in its intensity and the sun had set leaving the sky with a twinkling array of stars. It was pretty but I couldn't appreciate it, not when everything hinged on me getting Sir Axis to help us.

He paused outside an open doorway. "Here we are, gorgeous."

I firmed my lips. "Why couldn't my friend come inside with me?"

"My rules. He'll be fine. Nerita will give him the same treatment as you."

I narrowed my eyes. "What do you mean?"

"A room to refresh yourself and a change of clothes," he said. "Whatever else do you think I mean?"

His eyes glittered with mischievousness making my chest tighten even more at being away from Malachi. I hoped he was all right, but the jealous pit of despair welled inside me again.

Sir Axis's lips stretched into an all-knowing smile. I brushed past him and into the room then without further ado shut the door in his face. His deep chuckle reverberated through the timber door. I spun into the room and stomped over to the window. Outside the stars reflected on the great expanse of water surrounding the house in dozens upon dozens of white lights. A light fog hovered in the distance still covering the rest of the buildings we'd seen briefly. The water rippled as a tail breeched the surface. I flung open the windowpanes and leaned over the edge trying to glimpse the creature who'd swam past me. The unusual tail didn't breech the surface again, and I slumped against the window wishing

I'd escape into the night with Malachi and didn't have to worry about anything at all.

A knock clanged on the door, and I rushed over to fling it open. A small girl stood before me holding a dress draped over her arms. The material shone as though powered by magic itself. Hues of blues glistened from the folded material, she shifted, revealing layers of material that glistened in hues of purples and greens much like the tail I'd seen disappear into the water. As she walked further into the room and laid the dress on the bed, sparkling silver material fluffed from the mountains of fabric underneath the top skirts. Each layer of fabric appeared to hold a different color but there was also a magical quality to the dress that suggested the material was also shifting colors. It was an exquisite dress and nothing like I'd pick for myself to wear.

The girl hurried from the room as though I might harm her. I closed the door behind her, flicked the lock, and walked to the bed. For the first time since I'd stepped into the room, I noticed how beautiful it was. The bed appeared to float above the floor. They'd decorated it in swaths of luxurious fabric. When I touched it, the material was like living liquid running between my fingers. Behind the bed sat a wall made of water. The turquoise-blue water was so clear if there hadn't been a wall on the other side, I'd have peered through it.

I wished Malachi was with me to see the beauty of the room, but he was probably in a similar room in another house with Nerita. Why did I care so much if he'd found what we all wanted? I crossed to the window and shut it again sealing myself into the fate of dressing up for the Water Sprite Master. If this was his kingdom, then why didn't they call him King?

And how did he know my parents?

If I had to wear a dress to get the answers to my questions, then that's what I'd do. Besides, I couldn't stand the human material on my skin any longer. It itched and chafed. I found a door leading to a bathroom and gasped at the giant bathtub. It was already full of steaming water. I guess Sir Axis had phenomenal power over water and could easily fill a bathtub in seconds. The pretty floral scent coming from the water didn't make me question it too much. As though lured by the call of the water, I stripped my clothes and climbed into the bathtub. Bottles of creamy liquids lined the edge. I popped the cork and sniffed the contents one by one and found them all to be a lovely flowery aroma that I was eager to wash with. I lathered and rinsed until every inch of my skin smelled as good as the bath water.

The water was so decadent I thought I might stay in it all night and sleep, but there was too much to do. I surged out of the water. Time to get Sir Axis to help us. I dried myself with the baby blue towel I found folded on the shelves. There was an assortment of glass bottles on another shelf. Curious, I opened the lid to one and sniffed the contents. An exotic aroma wafted from the jar. The notes teased my senses and made my head surge with the exquisite loveliness. I dipped my finger into the jar and rubbed the cream over every inch of my body. My head swam even more with the scent.

Feeling relaxed, I pranced out of the bathing room and fingered the material of the dress. It was as exotic as the scent permeating from my skin. I shimmied the dress over my head, letting the material fall over my naked body. It brushed against my skin in a sensual slide that made every inch of my body inflamed. I flicked the skirts out and spun around letting the fabric fall back against my legs.

Some part of my mind realized I shouldn't be acting so happy in this dress, but the scent and the material were so luxurious. It was like all my problems had floated away once I had put them on. With an airiness I'd never experienced before, I flung open the door and sashayed down the stairs. The floating slats made it seem like I was flying, or swimming since they made some walls with the same panel of water as the bedroom.

Sir Axis stood at the bottom of the stairs. He'd changed clothes and was now dressed in a floaty cobalt blue shirt that was unbuttoned to his waist and left the broad expanse of his bronzed chest on display. A medallion hung from his neck, and he twirled it around with his fingers, keeping my gaze fixed on his flesh. Each spin of the disc drew me closer until I stopped on the step above him.

"You're exquisite," he said.

I lifted my hand and touched the medallion. A spark shot into my fingertips, and I dropped it against his chest.

"What was that?"

"Hmm, this old thing?" He lifted the sparkling medallion again. "It was a gift from a friend."

"It zapped me."

He cocked his eyebrow. "Fascinating."

"What does it mean?"

He shrugged, dropped the medallion, and held out his hand. "Beats me. It's never zapped me or any of my other lovers."

"Lovers?" I curled my hands into fists and stepped past him onto the floor.

"No one else gets close enough to touch it."

Did he mean he wanted us to be lovers? I peered over my shoulder. He was strikingly attractive, I had to admit to myself even though I wouldn't tell him I thought he was good looking. Sir Axis seemed cocky enough without me adding to his ego. His gaze caught mine, and he winked. The weird vibe I had from him had vanished after the bath. I flung my head around, my mind swam, and the edges of my eyes blurred into a delightful haze as I swayed on my feet.

His hands caught me and steadied me until the swaying sensation passed.

I touched a hand to my head. "I don't understand what's wrong with me."

"Nothing at all. The perfumed delights of the bath helped ease your worries." He tucked my arm through his. "Allow me to escort you to the festivities."

"Festivities?" I frowned. Worries? What was I supposed to be worried about? The perfumed lotion filled my senses with every inhale. Wasn't I meant to be doing something?

"Yes, the party has already started. It's not every day we get visitors, and not every day we get visitors with as much beauty as you and your friend."

Malachi! How had I forgotten him?

Sir Axis led me to the door. It opened before we arrived at it, and I noticed the young girl holding it open.

"Who is she?" I asked as we stepped through the door.

"Young Vanya."

"She looks different."

"Because she is."

"You don't like giving information, do you?"

He smiled and the effect on me made my legs wobble, but his arm kept me upright and moving toward the lights and sounds coming from a building in the distance. Our footsteps were soft on the timber walkway as though the water surrounding us muted the noise. The gentle swish of water lapped at the posts holding us up.

"Not to strangers who enter my kingdom when it should be impenetrable. Yet here you are."

"Why don't you want anyone in? Did humans kill your people too?"

That's right I was here to ask for his help to save our Spring of Life. The fresh air outside had eased the perfumed delights filling my head.

"More questions." He tutted.

"And more no answers." I shook my head.

Perhaps I'd wasted my time coming here if he was only willing to go around in circles whenever I asked a question.

"Sir Axis," I said grinding my feet to a stop. "I, we, need your help to fix our spring."

"Interesting," he said.

"What is?"

"You." He drew me closer toward him and for a moment my pulse spiked. Nerves ran through me. Did he want us to be lovers? Would this be the only way he'd help us? I don't think I had it in me to sell my body. He wasn't bad looking.

He wasn't Malachi.

Even though Malachi was only my friend.

I closed my eyes and waited for the inevitable kiss. One other Fae back home had kissed me. Curiosity had gotten the better of me, but I'd never experienced a great deal in that kiss. I didn't see what the fuss was about.

"Ciara, Ciara." He sighed. "What am I to do?"

I snapped my eyes open.

"Help us. You can, can't you?"

CHAPTER SEVENTEEN
MALACHI

NERITA HAD FLUTTERED ABOUT me the entire time I'd been in this place. Her attention had kept me focused on her and not the fact they had separated me from Ciara. I should never have let her go into the Water Sprite Master's house alone, but I didn't have a choice. We needed his help. He was our last hope.

The house Nerita had taken me to was charming, and she'd insisted I bathe and dress more fittingly for their realm. Not wanting to insult her, I did as she asked as quickly as possible because the scent coming from the bath water was so pleasant it made me want to stay in the bathroom and forget everything. Once I'd dressed in a flowing teal shirt and tight black pants, she led me to this enormous building. It was a vast ballroom floating in the middle of their village. Twinkling blue lights hung from the ceiling above the timber beams above our heads. The Water Sprites filled round tables seating a dozen people at each with blooming flowers, gold plates, and silver cutlery. They chatted amongst themselves as they devoured the plates of food on the tables.

Nerita insisted I sit at a table with her. The rest of the table was empty though, and I scanned the room looking for Ciara. Where was she? Was she all, right?

"Drink. Eat." Nerita slid a glass and a plate toward me.

"No thank you."

My stomach was tied in knots not knowing where Ciara was. The thought of eating when she might be in danger didn't sit well with me.

Nerita scowled. "The Master won't be happy."

I flicked my gaze toward her. She was beautiful. Her flowing hair cascaded down her back in soft waves. Her eyes were alight with desire. She had plush lips she kept licking with her tongue. It would be easy to kiss her. Lose myself in what she was offering. Her come-on was blatant enough, but all I'd think about was Ciara. I didn't want to kiss anyone but her. We'd once kissed other Fae in the Summer Court after daring each other to do it when we were young. I didn't like it then, so I knew I wouldn't like it now.

The room quietened. Every head turned toward the door. I followed the directions and at long last saw Ciara. Dia, she was beautiful. She took my breath away as she walked into the room on the Water Sprite Master's arm. The colorful dress swirled like a living eddy of water about her body. I couldn't tear my gaze away from her even if I wanted to.

"Looks like the Master has a new toy," Nerita said.

I scowled. No one would treat Ciara like a toy. She was a princess and deserved to be treated like one. People should bow at her feet. Worship her.

Each step carried her closer to me and my heart pounded harder, faster. I rose from the chair.

"Are you all right?" I asked.

"I'm fine." She squashed her lips together and glared at Nerita.

If she'd been my mate, then I would have let my imagination run wild she was jealous I was with another woman.

"Good. What are we doing here?" I directed my question to Sir Axis.

He drew a chair away from the table and motioned for Ciara to sit. She did so and the fact another man did that for her made my blood boil. I shoved my hands into the pockets of the black pants to hide the fact my power had glowed in my fingertips.

"You're meeting with me," Sir Axis said, sliding out of the chair beside Ciara and sitting at the table.

I scowled and reclaimed my seat. "At a party?"

He smirked. "Wherever I say. This is my kingdom. These are my people you've put in jeopardy by coming here and I'll do whatever I see fit is necessary to protect them."

Nerita clapped her hands as though his words deserved applause. Around us, the conversation started again. Perhaps she'd signaled for the party to recommence.

"We don't mean your people any harm," Ciara said.

"But you discovered a way in. If one comes, so will others."

"My brother and his mate traveled here before us, but your darts prevented them from venturing beyond the statues," she said.

"Your brother was the one who attempted to enter recently?"

"Aye."

"Young Lorcan? I remember the time he and your sister Saoirse snuck into one of my balls when we used to live in the Everglades many years ago."

"No, Rian."

"Ah, the heir to the throne. Interesting, he'd put himself in jeopardy. I'm sure your father had a lot to say on the matter."

"Father isn't himself."

The pain in her eyes hit me like a slash to the heart.

Sir Axis rested his arm behind the back of Ciara's chair and the empty one beside him. It was as though he was marking her as his. Surely, he wasn't her fated mate? If he was, there wasn't anything I could do about it.

A server in very little clothing hovered at the edge of the table. Sir Axis clicked his fingers, and she rushed forward. He said something to her, but my focus was on Ciara. The server hurried away and in what was only seconds, she returned with a tray of unusual beverages. Tall glasses rose from the silver tray. The liquid inside was a glowing blue and from the top, a mist rolled down the sides of the drinks, onto the tray, and over her hand. She placed a glass in front of the four of us one at a time and smiled at Sir Axis. The smile could only be described as sultry. She wiggled her rear end as she walked away confirming my suspicion she was flirting with Sir Axis.

"To new friendships," Sir Axis said, lifting the glass into the air.

Ciara's expression didn't look too sure, but she lifted her glass. I wrapped my hand around the one in front of me. The mist drifted over my hand and curled around my fingers.

"Is this a potion?" I asked.

"Smart young man you have here, Princess."

"What does it do?" Ciara asked ignoring his comment about me, which smarted a bit since she was always smarter than me.

"A little of this. A little of that." He smirked.

She rolled her eyes. "Enough with no answers. I'm not drinking unless I understand what it does."

Nerita smirked too. "Nothing bad will happen. Trust us."

"I'm sorry." Ciara shook her head. "But we don't know you."

"Yes, I know your parents. Your mother used to sing at my balls in the Everglades. Your father used to accompany her. They trusted us." Sir Axis peered into Ciara's eyes. "I miss our old kingdom of the Everglades. The Trappers hurt a lot of people when they attacked the Fae."

I wanted to dig his eyes out with the spoon on the table sitting beside my hand.

"Then you should trust us enough to tell us what is in the potion."

Sir Axis sighed. "Such is the drama." He clicked his fingers in the air and the lights dimmed. Above our heads tiny particles of luminous blue floated, and I did not comprehend what they were. "Very well, I'll tell you. It's a happy potion. It makes you happy. Free to do whatever you wish."

"That doesn't sound bad," Ciara murmured peering into her glass. "And you'll consider helping us?"

I wanted all those things for her, but drinking a potion wasn't the answer to our problems.

"It's not bad," he said inclining his head. "Most find it good."

Most? I was about to ask, but Ciara sipped the potion before the word escaped my mouth.

She licked her lips and said, "It tastes like blueberry."

"They are your favorite, no?"

"Aye," she said with a smile.

Damn, the Water Sprite Master for making her smile. Was it the potion already working on her? Or was she happy this man was her fated mate? If he was, I still wasn't sure what was going on between them.

Nerita placed her hand on my arm. "Drink up, handsome."

Her palm slithered up my arm and nudged my elbow. Ciara nodded at me, so I picked up the drink and placed the lip of the misty glass to my mouth. We shouldn't be doing this. We should ask for their help. Nerita urged my elbow upward until the liquid hit my lips. They tickled as though a feather was being traced over them. I opened my lips and let the liquid fill my mouth. Delicious flavors exploded over thousands upon thousands of tastebuds on my tongue.

"See, blueberry," Ciara said.

I nodded but didn't tell her the glass I held tasted the way I'd always imagined her to taste. Desire swamped me so much that I tipped the glass up and gulped the entire contents in one go as my cock throbbed an insistent beat in my pants to take Ciara in my arms and pleasure her until she was truly happy.

Sir Axis laughed and clapped his hands in delight. "Wonderful. Let's see where the evening takes us now."

Wait. What had I done?

CHAPTER EIGHTEEN

CIARA

I GIGGLED THEN SLAMMED a hand over my mouth. Since when did I giggle? The sensations running through my body from one sip of the happy potion made me feel light and airy. As if I didn't have a care in the world. In the back of my mind, I grasped I did, but I couldn't seem to conjure the will to let that into the front of my mind to be the thought I cared about right at this moment.

The server returned with another tray of drinks, but I shook my head and nursed the one I already held in my hand. Sir Axis and Nerita accepted the second drink, but Malachi didn't take another glass either. Neither of them told us to take the second drink which I was glad of because my head was floating in the clouds, or the water of this place. It was light and magical.

Soon musicians walked onto the stage and the strumming of instruments began. Sir Axis rose and bowed while offering me his hand.

"It would be my pleasure to dance with you."

I should deny him, but it was only a dance. What harm would happen from a dance? Mother and Father had been his friends once from what he said. I placed my hand in his and let him lead me onto the dance floor. He twirled me around and then drew me tight into his arms. A gasp of delight left my mouth as he floated us around the dance floor. I had to admit I was having fun dancing. Sir Axis was a fabulous dancer. At the end of the song, he twirled us back to the table. I fell into the chair out of breath from how many dips and twirls he'd entertained me with.

The moment I saw Malachi's expression though, the smile on my face dropped. His brows were in a deep furrow. His lips turned down. And the way he had his hands shoved under the table suggested he was struggling with his power. I thought the potion was supposed to make him happy.

"Come on, handsome," Nerita said. "Your turn to take me for a spin."

Malachi shoved his chair back and stomped onto the dance floor.

"I thought the potion made everyone happy?" I asked Sir Axis.

He lounged back in his chair with a smug grin on his face. "It does, but the person has to want to be happy for it to work."

"Are you saying Malachi doesn't want to be happy?" I turned to the dance floor.

Malachi placed one hand on Nerita's hip, the other he curled around her palm then he stepped them into a ballroom dance we'd learned through reading the human books. Nerita smiled and flowed with him. With each step, she drew closer to Malachi until their groins were brushing against each other. Jealousy pounded hard inside me. She must be his fated mate for him to dance with her like that because now she had her arms wrapped around his neck and her face close to his. Within kissing distance.

I rubbed my temples and then stood. "I can't be here."

Sir Axis laughed as I fled from the room, shoving past all the cheerful people in the place. I'd never been more out of place. More out of tune with everything in the world, but this wasn't our world. Father had it right when he locked us inside the Summer Court. The rest of the realms were too painful to bear.

Faster and faster my legs paced until I was running through the doors of the ballroom and outside onto the walkway hovering over the water. I clung to the railing and hauled in as much oxygen as possible.

The door creaked open and then closed, but I didn't want to talk to anyone. Didn't want to admit I'd never be happy without Malachi in my life.

"Ciara?" Malachi whispered.

"I'm fine," I said.

"You don't seem fine since we got here." He stepped closer and leaned on the railing beside me, peering into the dark water too. "I'm not either."

"You're not?" I whipped my head up.

"No." He turned his head sideways, and we were so close if I shifted a fraction, we'd be kissing.

I sucked in a breath and held it.

His gaze dipped to my mouth then he slammed his eyes shut. I thrust off the railing and put distance between us because surely I'd imagined the blatant lust in his eyes. Malachi didn't feel that way for me.

"Do you think we'll find our fated mates?" I asked.

His arms slipped on the railing as he forced himself to stand. "Why would you ask?"

I shrugged. "We in all probability have limited time to live, and Father waited two hundred years for Mother. We're both past that age now and we still haven't found ours. Or have you?"

"What are you talking about?" He frowned.

"Nerita. Is she your fated mate?"

"Dia, no. I couldn't imagine anyone worse for fate to send to me." He chuckled.

"You seemed happy dancing with her."

"You appeared happy dancing with Sir Axis," he shot back. "Is he your fated mate? Is that why you're asking? Is this your way of telling me?"

"No," I scoffed. "I was happy after drinking the potion. I was floating across the dance floor."

"You looked exquisite," he whispered.

The tension I'd experienced since coming to this realm tightened. My entire skin heated from head to foot. I shook the reaction away as an after-effect of the potion.

"Children," Sir Axis said as he flung open the door. "The party is inside, please join us, otherwise..."

"Otherwise, what?" I folded my arms over my chest.

"You can leave." He copied my stance.

Shite, we couldn't leave without coming for what we needed. I had to follow the Master's instructions. I wouldn't risk our last hope because I was jealous of Nerita and the way she'd danced with Malachi.

"We'll stay," Malachi said, holding out his hand for me.

The second he placed his palm in mine, triumph surged deep inside me. I was still his. He hadn't found his fated mate. I would spend every minute with him before he tossed me aside for a mate. Not that I thought he would. No, Malachi would insist on us being friends still even though seeing him with another woman would make me go insane.

Sir Axis opened the door for us. "Oh, I have a request for the princess."

"What else do you need me to do before you'll help us?" I sighed.

"Sing."

"I don't sing." She firmed her lips.

"I'm sure you do. You have your mother's blood in you." He smiled and closed the door sealing us inside the beautiful ballroom once again.

This time though, it seemed like fate had sealed us inside.

CHAPTER NINETEEN
MALACHI

I'D NEVER HEARD CIARA sing in all our years together, she'd never even hummed a tune. Now Sir Axis said that, why hadn't she sung like her mother? She clasped her hand with mine as I walked her back to the table. There were now other people sitting at the table we hadn't met, but Sir Axis extracted Ciara from my hold and led her up onto the stage. With nothing else to do but sit, I did so. Nerita leaned onto my side and rubbed her hand up and down my arm. I politely placed my hand over hers and stopped her caress before putting her hand on the table and smothering it with my firm palm so she couldn't budge it. She huffed but then Sir Axis took the stage.

"Everyone we have a special performance tonight." He spread his arms wide. "Most of you will remember the songstress Niamh from many years ago and how she used to perform for us. Well, now we have the great honor of her daughter Ciara to sing for us tonight."

A round of applause broke out and whispers and murmurs rippled around the room. Ciara was gorgeous. A spotlight shone on her from a bright golden beam of light glistening from the middle of the luminous blue lights. The fabric of her dress shimmered as she walked to the center of the stage. Her silvery blonde hair darkened to a golden blonde reminding me of gold. The flowers of her crown appeared even brighter than normal. She whispered something to Sir Axis, and he smiled while Ciara didn't appear happy. So much for the happy potion.

She clasped her hands in front of her while Sir Axis left the stage and reclaimed his seat at the table with me and the others. With a click of his fingers, the musicians began playing again. Ciara opened her mouth and then closed it again.

I smiled at Ciara encouragingly and her gaze found mine through the crowd. Every time she gazed at me like that the rest of the world fell away. There were only the two of us.

This time she opened her mouth and let the words out.

"In the days of old,
The kingdoms shared,
The beauty and wisdom of the many.
In the days of old,
We frolicked in the fields,
Shared our love with all.
Until the day arose,
An enemy of Fae,

An enemy of us all.
Until the day arose,
We fled the realms,
Evil squashed our love.
The king decreed,
To seal us in,
To keep us safe.
The king decreed,
To protect us,
To love us with his grace.
We were happy,
In our kingdom,
Content in our love.
We were happy,
With our knowledge,
Protected and safe.
Then one day,
The Spring changed,
The magic less.
Then one day,
Our powers.
Not the same.
Our love,
Our hope,
Our existence,
Our choices,
Left us dying.
Choices made in love.
Our love for all,
Around us,

Our love for,

Family.

Friends.

Our fated mates."

Her voice was the sweetest sound I'd ever listened to in my life. My heart swelled inside my chest. She'd not only sung beautifully, but she'd sung a song with meaning. The song told a tale. Our tale. I was so proud of her. My applause was the loudest in the room. I stood and clapped even louder if that was possible. If only I could tell her how much she meant to me.

Ciara seemed to float down the stairs in her radiant gown, and I stepped toward her before she sat at the table, there was no way I wanted to share her with Sir Axis again.

"You were magnificent," I said.

She ducked her head, but I placed a finger under her chin and tilted her face upward again. Ciara deserved the attention, but I was selfish and wanted it to be from me.

"Dance with me?"

Her lips tilted up in a small smile. I slid my hand away from her face before I held onto it and plundered her lips with the raging desire running through me. Threading my fingers with hers, I led Ciara on to the dance floor. Around us, the Water Sprites danced to the music still filling the room from the musicians. Their tune had changed from one of melancholy to a softer, sweeter cadence. Once I paused, Ciara stepped closer to me and placed her other hand on my waist. I copied her pose, lifted our joined hands, and stepped into a waltz even though the music didn't suit the human steps.

Soon our steps changed with the music, became more fluid, more in sync with the tune as though the beats sunk into our very skin and danced our limbs. Our bodies drifted closer and closer until each step brought an agonizing torturous brush of her body against mine. I willed my cock to not react, but it stirred in my pants growing harder with each barely there touch. I curled my fingers tighter into her waist hoping she'd complain and make us stop, but she lifted her chin and gazed into my eyes with a question deep inside their blue depths.

The words of love hovered on my tongue, but I couldn't tell her. She deserved her fated mate. No matter how much I attempted to think of her as only a friend, my body had other ideas. The music changed and turned sultrier. Out of the corner of my eye, I glimpsed the Water Sprites writhing against each other on the dance floor, but the sight of the overtly sexual display didn't stop me from dancing with Ciara. She was the only one I cared about. I'd dance with her all night. All day. Every day.

She sighed and dropped her head to my chest laying it over the rapid beating of my heart. Could she hear how it beat for her? Could she sense I wanted her to be mine? Her hand slid from mine, and she wrapped both arms around me. We were so close now not even a piece of her beloved paper would fit between us. I gave into my desire and wrapped my other arm around her, giving into the dream they fated us as mates. As I swayed in time with her, I closed my eyes as the song ended and another started.

How many songs we danced through, I couldn't say, but without warning Ciara jerked out of my arms and placed one hand over her stomach, the other over her mouth.

"What's wrong?"

"Shite not now," she mumbled. "I need to get out of here."

Her scent which had engulfed me while dancing grew even more enticing. Even more alluring. My mouth watered for a taste of her.

"You're in heat," I said, knowing full well what that meant.

"Aye." She chewed on her bottom lip.

"Let's get you somewhere else. Somewhere safe." I wrapped an arm around her shoulders and walked her through the throng of Water Sprites who'd progressed from dancing to outright fornication on the dance floor. How had I not noticed? Because I'd been too wrapped up in dancing with Ciara for song after song unwilling to let her go. There was only ever her and to have her in my arms in any way was the most mind-blowing experience.

I led us to Sir Axis's table and found him lounging back in his seat with an amused smirk on his face. I wasn't a confrontational person, but my fingers curled of their own accord to punch him and wipe the smirk from his face.

"Well, if it isn't the 'friends'," Sir Axis drawled.

Ciara frowned. "I'm sorry to leave the festivities." She swept an arm around the room which had turned into an orgy while we'd been dancing for what could have been hours in our blissful state.

Not only was the dance floor full of semi-naked Water Sprite's fornicating, but so were the tables. On the table beside ours, they'd spread a woman across the tabletop while two men suckled on her nipples and a third pounded into her. The moans coming from the woman grew louder and louder until they grated on my nerves.

"You could always stay and join in." He cocked an eyebrow.

"The princess wishes to leave, so she will," I said.

"Ah, he has a backbone. I like it." Sir Axis stood. "Come with me."

"If you so much as put a hand on her," I threatened.

"That's for the princess to decide, is it not?" He stepped closer to us. "If I'm not mistaken, you sweet Ciara, are in heat and in desperate need of service."

"Don't talk to her like that," I said.

"It's the truth." He folded his arms over his chest. "Have no fear, you can give in to your body's demands tonight without the consequences that would without doubt occur if you were back home."

"What does that mean?" Ciara asked.

"The potion you drank earlier is also a contraception. Otherwise, we'd have too many of us running around here." He chuckled. "Besides it'd become incestuous after a time."

Ciara wrinkled her nose.

I agreed with her. While group sex wasn't anything I'd even contemplated, after seeing it in the flesh, I saw its appeal. But there would only ever be one woman for me, and she wasn't even the one destined for me.

"I can think of nothing worse." Ciara lifted her chin and met him head-on for attitude.

Dia, I loved her even more.

"Very well. Let me show you to a house where you'll be safe to weather your desires if that's what you wish."

"Aye."

His smirk dropped, but he led us out of the ballroom and into the much fresher air outside. Each inhale was easier, but I still smelled Ciara's heat. It didn't help that with every step she brushed against me and all I could think about was having her naked against my body.

Sir Axis rambled as we walked, but I couldn't concentrate on a word he said. He might have told us how to cure the spring for all I knew. I hoped Ciara was paying attention because I sure wasn't.

Each step across the boards took us deeper into the village. More and more houses appeared as the fog no longer surrounded them. Across the horizon of the water, the first sparkling rays of the sun rose into the radiant black sky. The twinkling stars diminished with every minute the sun rose higher and there were less and less to look at.

"Here we are," Sir Axis said stopping in front of a quaint timber board house. "You can wait out your heat inside this house. No one will bother you here."

"And we're to take your word for it?" I asked.

Perhaps we should leave and go back through the waterfall, but then what if her fated mate was a wolf shifter in the village below like her other two sisters? Was it wrong to want another day with her to myself even though I wouldn't be with her?

"My word is law here," Sir Axis said with so much authority I didn't even think to question him again.

"We'll be good here," Ciara said.

I whipped my head toward her. What did she mean by us? Didn't she appreciate how hard it was for me to be around her while she was in heat? It was why I'd left her alone in the Summer Court palace the other time she'd rode it out in solitude because she hadn't wanted to risk falling pregnant to another Fae. If she was worried about being in the house alone, then I'd be there for her, but my cock was already hard with wanting her before she was in heat and now...

No matter how much I already loved her and wanted her. Desired her to be mine in every way possible, then I'd shove those thoughts aside as best I could.

CHAPTER TWENTY

CIARA

MALACHI DIDN'T LOOK HAPPY about our current predicament, and I couldn't blame him. He probably wished he was with his fated mate while she was in heat and not babysitting his best friend. It wasn't as though he'd do anything without permission. Even if I dropped hints, he'd need me to ask before he'd act. Malachi was the best of the best. I trusted him with my life. And I trusted him with my heat. He'd take care of me. If I asked, he'd give me anything. But could I put him in that position as my best friend?

Sir Axis grinned. "Have fun. When you're ready, we'll talk."

I wanted to throttle him. I was ready to talk the moment we arrived. This song and dance we'd put on for him had been just that. Entertainment for the bored Water Sprite Master no doubt. I understood what it was like to have lived for hundreds of years in one place, and by the looks of it the Water Sprites had stayed secluded like us. But Sir Axis was older than me, older than my father from what he'd said about Mother singing at their balls. He comprehended a lot more than any of us too.

But while I focused on those thoughts, a fresh wave of my heat hit me. I placed a hand over my stomach trying to suppress the frenzy pounding inside my womb. It wanted to be filled. Why were Fae heats so dramatic? I'd spent years researching them after watching the way my older sisters struggled with lust and not having a fated mate. It seemed like a cruel twist we befell our heat before we found our mate.

I turned to Malachi. "I'm worried about being in there alone. What if someone gets in? What if..."

"No one will get in. I'll make sure of it." He strode toward the door. "Let me make sure no one is in there to start with."

"Malachi." I chased after him. "I don't want to be inside alone. This place isn't natural. I sense magic at play."

"I sense it too. We already comprehend they have a barrier like our Veil."

"There's more to it than that, but I can't put my finger on it. And then there's the way Sir Axis refuses to answer our questions. The way he gave us potions. Why would he do so if he didn't want us out of sorts?"

"You're right," he said. "I won't leave your side until we get out of here and back to the Summer Court."

He turned the intricately carved doorknob and opened the quaint timber door. The same luminescent blue that was inside the ballroom lit the room from the ceiling. We stepped inside and Malachi locked the door and tested it twice.

"This is adorable," I said.

The room was small, but the way they decorated it made it seem spacious. Perhaps it was the expanse of blue water running down the wall as though a waterfall was inside that made me connected to the small house. I walked toward the water, but a fresh wave of my heat hit me, and my legs shook so much I had to pause with one hand on the wall and the other flattened tight against my stomach.

Malachi rushed over to me but hovered with his hands clenching and unclenching by his side. "What can I do?"

I laughed hollowly as my gaze found his concerned face. The way his eyes lit with desire gave me hope, but the way his face then twisted made those hopes vanish into a puff of air.

"I... we..." he stuttered at a loss for words.

I'd never ask him to cross the line of friendship, but I'd thought there was more building between us while we'd been dancing. It must have been the happy potion Sir Axis foisted upon us.

I shoved off the wall and stormed through the next door and found a bedroom. As another wave of arousal hit me, I flung myself onto the bed and gripped the pillow in a tight embrace.

"Ciara?" Malachi said faintly from the doorway.

"Go away, Malachi."

"But you're in pain. I can't stand to see you in pain."

The anguish in his voice made me roll over and stare up at the thatched roof above my head. This was another cozy room filled with an enormous bed. I imagined they designed it for the way the Water Sprites appeared to take multiple lovers at once. The mattress was soft but firm beneath my back and my thoughts drifted to what it'd be like to be pounded into the mattress. I rubbed my legs together, but it only made the arousal running through me worse.

"It'll pass. It did last time." I groaned and rolled onto my side.

Malachi's footsteps echoed over the floorboards and then he was beside me taking my hand in his. He was always there for me holding my hand through the good and the bad. Tears welled in my eyes.

"Don't cry," he whispered.

"This is a mess," I whispered back.

"It's not your fault." He squeezed his fingers.

"But we're meant to be finding a cure and all I can think about is sex. What it would be like. How it would feel." My voice drifted out huskier than usual.

His gaze dropped to our hands. "I want to be here for you, but I don't think I can."

"What do you mean?" I inched closer toward him afraid he'd disappear, and I'd be alone. All alone.

"Your scent." He shook his head as if trying to clear it. "You always smell sweet, but right now every time I breathe in its filling my entire body with you."

"Great so now I smell."

He chuckled. "Not in a bad way. It's... delicious."

"Delicious like a juicy blueberry?" I asked.

He grinned. "Even better."

"Hmm, I didn't think there would be anything better for a Fae."

"Oh, there is, believe me." His gaze hit my face with the intensity of lust I was experiencing.

Silence descended between us as the air thickened with our desire.

"Malachi?"

"Ciara?"

We said at the same time then laughed.

"You go first," I said.

"I think I should wait in the other room."

Everything inside me shattered. "If that's what you want," I whispered through the thickness of my throat.

"It doesn't matter what I want. I have to do what's right."

He shifted, but I tugged on his hand not letting go and keeping him in place.

"What do you want?"

He shook his head and his throat bobbed as he swallowed hard. "I can't tell you, I love you too much."

"I love you too. It's important to me what you want."

He sighed and dropped his head onto the mattress. I reached out with my free hand and stroked his hair. A half moan half groan rumbled from him.

"Tell me," I pleaded. "We always tell each other everything. I don't like knowing you've kept a secret from me."

"I can't," he mumbled into the mattress. "You should—"

I tugged his hair, so he'd look at me and asked, "I should what?"

"You're a princess."

"So?"

"And I'm simply me."

"You're special."

"To you I am." He eased my hand from his hair and clasped both my hands in his.

"Isn't that enough?"

"I'm not sure." He dropped his gaze to our joined hands. "I guess when we find our fated mates, we'll be special to them too."

Desperate tears formed in my eyes, and I couldn't stop them. I wasn't sure if it was the potion or my heat, but I threw away my hesitation. We had each other and without a doubt, that was enough.

"I don't want to find mine," I said.

"What?" His head jerked up.

"I want you." I shuffled closer.

"You want me?" he asked as though the mere thought was incredulous.

"Aye. I love you, Malachi. You're my best friend. Always there for me. You understand me more than anyone else does."

"Your fated mate will do the same."

"No." I yanked his hands closer. "I. Want. You."

He shook his head. "You're saying that because you're in heat."

"I'm not." How would I make him understand? This love I had for him was more than anything else. "I've loved you all my life. Nothing will ever change my feelings for you."

"One day a man will come along, and he'll change them. You'll love him more." His voice cracked at the end.

"Go then." I let go of his hands. "You don't love me the way I love you."

"You couldn't be more wrong." He sat on the side of the bed.

"How? You admitted you'd rather wait for your fated mate."

"I never said that." He huffed. "I couldn't care less about who the fates send me. Ciara, I love you. I've wanted you for a long time, but you deserve to be happy. You deserve your fated mate."

"I would always be happy with you."

"You say that now..." He sighed.

I sat up. "I will always say that. There's nothing you can do that wouldn't make me happy. Unless you left me for another woman that is."

"I'd never leave you." He lifted a hand as though he was about to touch me then dropped it back to the mattress.

"I'd never leave you either."

I let out a long breath as though purging my feelings had lifted a great strain from my chest and the lightness inside me made my dark shadows easier to bear. Whenever I was with Malachi his mere presence soothed me. Now while I was in heat, I had the added sensation of his presence arousing me. I doubted I'd ever feel this way for another man. What I said was true. I'd never leave him. I loved him and only him. If my fated mate appeared one day, if we lived that long, then there was no chance I'd leave Malachi for a stranger. We had so much history together. How could he think I'd hurt him?

We stared at each other for a long time, both of us lost in our thoughts. My heat gnawed at me like the constant pressure of the water outside. My gaze dropped to his lips. Lips I longed to kiss. I wondered what it would be like to kiss Malachi. What sex with Malachi would be like?

"I've never had sex," he said.

"Neither have I. I didn't even like kissing someone else so I could never bring myself to try again let alone have sex with them."

"Remember when we found those books?"

"The anatomy ones or the secret manuals Eabha had hidden in the library on the top shelf?"

He grinned. "Both."

"We spent a long time pouring over those together."

"We did," he agreed. "So, we both understand how our bodies work."

"You're making it sound so technical."

"I don't want to disappoint you."

"Oh, Malachi. You would never disappoint me."

"And you're sure this isn't because of your heat."

I lifted a hand and cupped his cheek. "I'm one hundred percent sure my feelings for you aren't because of my heat. Since we've been on Earth, my body tingles whenever you touch me. That has nothing to do with my heat."

"I've always felt that way as though your presence lights up my body and my power."

"I realized the other day that I didn't just love you but that I was in love with you."

"I've been in love with you for what feels like forever."

Did that mean we were about to kiss? About to have sex for the first time? My heart hammered inside my chest and echoed the desire pounding deep in my core. If this was real, then I couldn't be happier, but if Malachi left the room, then my heart might break at losing what we might have had together.

CHAPTER TWENTY-ONE
MALACHI

I T WAS LIKE CIARA had ripped my thoughts and
feelings from my head and my heart. My pulse beat
a steady tempo inside my temple and in my rock-hard
cock. Her scent had made it near impossible to
concentrate on what she was saying, but I loved her
so much I'd do anything for her. I'd almost walked
out of the room when she'd told me to leave. But the
naked love bared on her face had kept me by her side.

If she wanted me, loved me, was in love with me
too, then who was I to say no to her?

I'd always do whatever she needed to make her
happy.

She needed me.

I leaned forward, and she sucked in a breath as though
the anticipation was too much for her. It was too much
for me. The number of times I'd fantasized about kissing
her was far too many for a best friend. She was always
more than that though. Ciara thought she was dark, but

she was my dark. She helped counteract the blaring light in my powers.

Light and dark.

The two needed each other.

Our breaths merged as I closed the distance millimeter by millimeter. I wanted to remember this moment for the rest of my life however long that would be. If we only had a human lifetime left, then I wanted those years to be full of Ciara. But I'd do my best to make sure we had many centuries together.

Her palm was light on my cheek. Her touch sent tiny shivers through my body. I closed the last of the distance between our mouths. Our lips connected. Power jolted through me. She gasped as though she'd experienced it too. The hot breath she'd let out lit a fire inside me. I didn't kiss her sweetly or gently like I'd planned. My lips took her mouth in a ravenous kiss. I'd kissed others before, but I'd never kissed like this. There had been no overwhelming desire with the other women I kissed to banish my feelings for my best friend. With Ciara, I was consumed by her. I loved it.

I eased her onto her back and laid my body on top of hers while still ravaging her mouth in a hungry, desperate kiss. Her lips were like honey, sweet and tasty. Her tongue was like my throbbing cock, urgent and insistent in my mouth. For a split second, I wondered who she'd learned to kiss like this from but then my power flared to my palms in a jealous rage, so I shoved the thought away. It didn't matter who either of us had kissed before, there was only us right here, right now.

She spread her legs and wrapped them around my waist. I groaned as the heat of her desire rubbed against my cock. She rolled her hips beneath me, so I joined her in the frenzied action without conscious thought of what we were doing.

This wasn't enough though. I needed all of her. I ripped my mouth from hers earning me a frustrated groan. As I attempted to sit up, she chased me, so I placed a hand on her chest and forced her back to the mattress.

"Wait," I panted. "I... we.... Naked."

She laughed but nodded. I stood in a hurry and undressed my shirt and pants. The Water Sprite material floated to the floor as though it were floating through water. Ciara shimmied out of her dress while still on the bed and the sight undone me to see her stripping for me. All of her was mine.

A delicate pink stained her cheeks when she saw me staring at her naked form, but I couldn't drag my gaze away from her. She was perfect from the tips of her tight pink nipples to the rounded flesh of her breasts, the curve of her waist, and the blonde curls at the apex of her legs where the scent of her heat was pouring into the air even more now. I licked my lips. I longed to taste every inch of her body. And I would.

I crawled back onto the bed and noticed her staring at my straining cock. It made it jump in response to the hungry expression on her face. I dropped a kiss on her forehead and then trailed my lips down the side of her face evading her mouth, otherwise, I'd become fused with her again and lost in the blazing inferno of our kiss.

"Malachi?"

"Hmm?" I mumbled against her skin.

"You're beautiful."

My lips smiled even as I kissed her neck.

"Thank you." I suckled on her neck which earned me an arch of her back. "You're more beautiful though."

As I reached her collarbone, I trailed tiny kisses across it before heading lower toward her breasts. Each kiss on her delicate skin made me want to mark it with love bites, but would she like that? There was only one way to find out. I opened my mouth and suckled the skin near her nipple.

"Oh, my," she gasped.

"Did you like that?"

"I did."

"What about this?" I closed my mouth around her nipple and lured the tight peak into the warmth of my mouth.

She cried out again and arched her back thrusting her breast closer to me. I took the invitation and sucked on her nipple harder, then harder still until her arms wrapped around my shoulders and her nails dug into my flesh.

"Aye," she said rubbing her thighs together.

I trailed a fingertip down her stomach and then paused. What if I did this wrong?

She grabbed my wrist and urged my hand between her spread legs. I'd experienced nothing like her before.

What we'd read in books paled against real life. She was slick. My finger glided over her flesh and the more I stroked my finger, the more she moaned. I needed to see what she liked, so I shifted lower on the bed until I was lying between her spread thighs.

"What are you... doing?" She gasped again as I rolled my finger over her flesh.

"I'm figuring out what I need to do for you to enjoy this."

"Believe me, I'm enjoying anything you do."

"Not good enough, Ciara." I tsked. "You deserve the best."

"So do you." She clung to the sheets. "You haven't let me touch you."

"Later. You're the one in heat."

I turned my attention back between her legs letting my finger glide over the hard nub at the top that was the tip of her clitoris. Touching it was supposed to make her aroused, and it appeared to be doing the trick because her breathing was becoming erratic. Arousal seeped from her entrance, and I couldn't resist the temptation to gather it up on my finger and taste it. An explosion of headiness hit my tongue. I wanted to drink it every day and I would from now on. If she ever found her fated mate, then I'd kill him to keep her for myself.

My finger dropped back to her soaked entrance and traced where I'd bury my cock. Her hips rocked side to side following my finger. Ciara's skin grew flushed and glistened with moisture. Her nipples were so tight they seemed painful. I lifted my other hand to pinch one between my thumb and finger.

"Dia," she groaned. "I need you inside me."

"Like this?" I asked sliding my finger into her dripping entrance that I'd been rimming.

"Aye." She rolled her hips downward to take more than the tip of my finger.

She was so warm and wet. I closed my eyes for a second letting this moment sink in. I was inside Ciara. Closer than we'd ever been. Her walls were tightly gripping my finger and my cock throbbed wanting to experience it too. My eyes snapped open. I couldn't wait a moment longer. To have her as mine. Too much like all my dreams come true. I crawled up the bed keeping my finger buried deep and I kissed her again.

Ciara returned my kiss with the heat of an inferno. She was burning up and taking me with her. I didn't care. I'd go anywhere with her. Her hips rolled beneath me making my finger thrust in and out of her with no effort from me. That wouldn't do. If that was the motion she desired, then that was what she'd get from me.

I withdrew my hand making Ciara huff as though she hated me leaving her. I wasn't leaving. Merely changing how I'd be inside her. This was it. We were about to lose our virginity to each other. My best friend and the woman I loved. I coated my cock with her arousal, then held the base as I guided it between her legs. She opened her thighs even wider urging me on to take her. Own her. Make her mine in a way I shouldn't. I couldn't stop now even if her fated mate walked through the door.

The blunt tip of my cock touched her warm flesh, and I groaned from the slight contact. She held her breath as though this moment was bigger than both of us. Bit by bit I eased inside her until I had to shift my hand out of the way. She let out her breath and I thrust the rest of the way inside.

"Are you all right?" I asked.

"Aye."

"I didn't hurt you?"

"Never." She lifted her head and kissed me.

It broke my restraint. Nature or instinct took over and my hips plunged thrusting my cock along her tight walls. Each surge of our bodies coming together had never been so right. She wrapped her legs around my waist taking me even deeper. Her hands clung to my shoulders. My tongue slid against hers as our mouths couldn't part for even a second on this momentous occasion. I never dreamed it would be this good. My balls tightened as the pleasure grew too much. Her walls squeezed against my thrusting cock, so each slide was more pleasurable than the last.

Ciara's breathing grew erratic. I'd never experienced a woman's orgasm, but I wanted to experience Ciara's. I shoved back my pleasure for a moment, slid my hands under her back, and drew her body closer to mine. Her moans grew louder now as though being closer to me was what she needed.

Deep inside her muscles tightened and tightened until she exploded. Contractions of her orgasm squeezed my cock, and I followed her into ecstasy. My eyes rolled back in my head. Blood pounded inside my ears as my heart pounded so hard, I thought I might pass out from sheer pleasure. Ciara's hands gripped me harder against her, then she ripped her mouth from mine and drew in a ragged breath.

I'd never in my life experienced anything like this. Happy didn't even cover it. Euphoric maybe wasn't enough. Out of the blue, my power throbbed as though it wanted me to mark her as my mate, but I couldn't do that. She might change her mind about me when she met the real man destined for her. I'd love her and pleasure her for as long as she'd have me.

Then I'd die of a broken heart when she left me, for I was sure she would put a fated mate before me even though she said otherwise. I appreciated how much she revered her parent's relationship. There was no way she'd give up having a fated mate even for me.

Her legs dropped from my waist, and I lowered her back to the mattress before little by little leaving her body even though I didn't want to, and my cock was still semi-hard.

Ciara smiled at me with love shining in her eyes and it chased away the dark thoughts.

"You... we..."

She laughed. "We should have been doing this for years."

CHAPTER TWENTY-TWO
CIARA

MALACHI LAUGHED AND KISSED me hard on the lips. "Dia, I love you so much."

He stood and scanned the room.

"What are you looking for?" I was too boneless from having sex for the first time to even move.

"The bathing chambers."

"Come back here." I held my hand out and wiggled my fingers.

His gaze dipped between my legs. "I want to clean you first."

"I enjoy knowing I'm messy from you." My cheeks heated as I spoke the words. This was so different, but it felt right.

He leaned over me. "I love knowing I was the first inside you. The first to make you messy."

"First and last," I said leaning forward to kiss him.

I caught his lips with mine and sunk into the instant connection of our mouths. His lips roamed over mine languidly as though taking his time to learn every curve to them. He broke the kiss and rested his forehead against mine a moment before shoving off and striding from the room. I sunk back on the mattress and grinned with the glow of our pleasure. Even in daylight, strange blue lights fluttered around the house. My inquisitive side who wanted to comprehend everything made a note to research everything about the Water Sprites when we returned.

Malachi strode back into the room with a towel in his hands. The look on his face flittered between rapt awe and feral lust as his gaze skittered over my naked body from head to toe. My gaze did the same thing. Every inch of his body was a piece of art. If I were like my sister Roisin, then I'd paint him on a canvas, so I'd stare at Malachi all day long. His arms were muscular, more so than I'd ever pictured they would be beneath his clothes. Veins ran up his forearms and wrapped around his biceps. I knew he trained in sword fighting with his father but seeing the display of strength in those arms made me swoon.

I trailed my gaze across the column of his throat and down his chest. What would it be like to mark him as my mate? To see my mark on his chest. My power swirled to my hands coating my palms and twining up my wrists. Heat curled low again as a fresh wave of my heat consumed me. Lower my gaze traveled soaking in the sight of Malachi standing naked before me. His stomach muscles were as well defined as his arms and my mouth watered to run my tongue over every inch and valley. I wanted to see if he'd enjoy my lips and tongue on his body the way I'd enjoyed his on mine.

Then my gaze found the straining hard length of his cock. A drop of pearlescent cum formed on the tip. That same cum was now inside me and I squeezed my legs together as though I'd be able to keep it forever. If it wasn't for the potion Sir Axis gave us, then we would have made a baby. The thought didn't repulse me. It turned me on even more. To have a permanent connection between us would have made this night even more special. I regretted drinking the potion, but I couldn't undo it. I would only go forward from here and that was with Malachi as more than my friend.

He was now my lover, and I needed him now deep inside me again.

"Can I taste you like you did me?" I asked.

His eyebrows rose but then he strode toward the bed stopping only once his thighs hit the mattress. I lifted a hand and swiped my finger through the cum beading the tip of his cock. Tentatively I placed my finger in my mouth. Malachi's essence hit my tongue like an added aphrodisiac. I leaned forward and ran my tongue along his cock then I shifted onto my knees and did what I'd imagined moments ago and kissed and licked my way across his tight abdominal muscles, higher to the tiny tips of his nipples where I flicked my tongue over each one.

He groaned. "You're torturing me."

"We can't have that." I smiled as I kissed up his jaw and found his mouth once again.

His hand caressed my back in long strokes, sending goose bumps over my skin. The hard touch of his naked chest against my nipples made them ache even more than they already were. His hands drifted downward with each caress until they were smoothing over my buttocks and ratcheting up my lust. More moisture gathered between my legs, and we'd both forgotten the towel Malachi had carried into the room with him. I didn't need cleaning when I wanted him to make me messy again right now.

But Malachi had other ideas than the ones running through my head. He broke our kiss and put his hand between us holding the towel and with sure strokes, he wiped our previous joining from between my legs. But I was so aroused I couldn't take the sweet gesture for what it was as the towel rubbed against my sensitive, inflamed skin. I gasped as more blood pooled to my core with the touch that wasn't supposed to be erotic, but it was. Everything Malachi did turned me on.

"Ciara," he groaned my name like I was a miracle and dropped the towel on the floor.

His fingers found my core and filled me with the swirl of two fingers deep inside me. They hit a spot and made my legs quiver.

"If I remember the anatomy books right, this is your g-spot."

"Oh," I moaned as his fingers rubbed until all the muscles in my body lit in pleasurable fire. It coursed through my veins and returned to the spot. Everything vanished apart from the magic of his fingers inside me.

He dipped his lips to the shell of my ear and whispered, "Are you going to orgasm from this?"

Was I? Is that what this intense sensation was? The build of an orgasm. The one I'd experienced while having sex with him had been like I was in another universe. There had only been our bodies moving in sync to completion. This was different. This was Malachi producing my pleasure.

"Perhaps," I whispered as I shuddered against him.

My legs quivered and threatened to collapse under me. He wrapped an arm around my waist and held onto me. The tip of his hard cock nudged my stomach, and I longed for him to fill me with it again. To take his magic fingers away, but then his fingers made the pending orgasm explode and all I could do was gasp and moan as deep inside me the pulsating pleasure sent me to the stars and the moon.

"Aye, you did," he said sounding proud he'd figured out a way to make me come.

I dropped my head on his shoulder. "I can't describe the way you make me feel. It's too intense."

His palm rolled against my mound and a sudden sharp throbbing surged from the hard tip of my clitoris.

"Oh, Dia."

"More?"

"Aye." I brushed my lips on his chest over his heart. The place where I wanted to mark him. My powers hadn't abated during my orgasm and now they surged even more to my hands, but I couldn't mark him here otherwise we'd fall into the Quiet for who knows how long. We had to cure the Spring first. If we could...

If Malachi even wanted me to mark him.

He removed his hand and slid his cock home. For he was my home, and I hoped I was his. We'd always be each other's home.

His hands cupped my buttocks as he slid in and out of me. Our chests squashed together. Our hearts pounded. The pleasure of being this close to Malachi again made every nerve in my body sing with desire. Our bodies grew slick with sweat but neither of us cared. All we cared about was each other and the pleasure we enjoyed in each other's arms.

Our breathing grew ragged. Malachi's thrusts grew more erratic. The pleasure coursing through my body drove me to the pinnacle, and I clung to him as I tumbled over the edge into the freefall of bliss with the one man I trusted. Malachi kept moving through my orgasm making my head spin into new heights of ecstasy and then he came deep inside me sending a fresh wave of pleasure running through me.

This was the man I loved more than anything.

I wanted him to be mine forever.

CHAPTER TWENTY-THREE
MALACHI

S PENDING AN ENTIRE DAY loving Ciara, how I'd longed
for such a long time had been the happiest day of
my life and that was saying something because I was
always happy when I was with her. She made my heart
whole and now she'd made my body whole. We'd talked
between rounds of sex. Eaten the bowl of fruit we'd
found in the kitchenette then I'd eaten Ciara for the first
time spread across the countertop. She'd tasted better
than the sweet fruit, but then I always knew she would.

Her heat and the potion, so she wouldn't fall
pregnant, was a brief reprieve from the coming tragedy
of our lives.

As the sun set and the heady aroma of Ciara's heat
shifted into her sweeter scent, we both understood we
couldn't put off the inevitable any longer. We washed in
the bathing room, taking the time to clean each other
with the perfumed soap. Our hands glided over each
other's bodies as though we hadn't spent an entire day

worshipping each other. Her touch still turned me on, but I willed my cock to not harden to full mast.

Stepping out of the bathroom we dried and found an armoire with an assortment of clothes. Ciara shimmied on a black dress with gold threads glistening under the blue lights from above. She seemed even more magical. I dressed in a pair of dark pants and a tight shirt of starry night blue which clung to my chest.

I took her hand in mine and led her toward the door.

"Malachi, wait." She jerked my hand.

I stopped and raised my eyebrow.

Her pretty pink tongue which had done wicked things to my body darted out along her lips.

"I want you to know—"

I placed a finger over her lips. She didn't need to tell me. "I understand."

She nodded, and I dropped my hand. I recognized she loved me. She realized I loved her. That was all that mattered.

I opened the door, and we stepped outside into the fresh air of the Water Sprites' village. They'd hidden away their secret place from the rest of the world. They were like us.

A girl rushed forward. "Sir Axis is awaiting you."

"I remember you," Ciara said. "You were at Sir Axis's house."

"I was." She strode along the walkway making us rush to keep up with her. For such a small thing she sure was fast.

"Are you his daughter?" Ciara asked.

"Heavens no." She laughed. "I'm not even a Water Sprite."

"What are you then?" I asked.

She lifted the thick length of her hair away from her ear and revealed its pointed tip.

"You're an Elf!"

"I've never met an Elf," Ciara said. "I've met no one but Fae until recently."

The girl flicked her hair back into place.

"I have to say, I'm enjoying our trip." I grinned.

Ciara blushed because she understood I meant our time together alone. "Me too," she whispered.

The girl led us from the boardwalks over the water and onto the rich soil. At once a jolt of power shot up through my bare feet. My palms glowed a radiant white. Ciara too must have sensed the connection because her shadows were covering her hands and twining around her wrists.

Sir Axis sat at the edge of the forest on a throne carved from a large log of a Redwood tree stretching to the sky behind him. The closer we stepped the more I made out the intricate carvings on the throne. Swirls depicting water leaped from the armrests. They'd carved water creatures into the legs and behind his head were the wings of a gigantic bird.

"Ah, the 'friends' are gracing me with their presence."

Ciara tilted her chin high not letting his comment get to her. She was so strong. I admired that about her. I wouldn't take his dig either.

"We are friends," I said.

His fingers tapped on the arm. "Friends who fuck."

Ciara gasped. The girl ran into the woods as though she didn't want to be here for this.

"What Ciara and I do, is our business." I folded my arms over my chest.

"True." He lounged back on his throne and flung a leg over his knee. "So, what do you want to ask, Princess Ciara?"

Ciara stepped forward. "Sir Axis, we'd like to thank you for your hospitality."

He nodded.

"We have an enormous problem in the Summer Court. Our Spring of Life is languishing and will soon cease to flow. If that happens, we'll lose our immortality. The Fae will die." She forced her palms together and her powerful shadows vanished. "We've searched for a cure but have found none. Since you're exceedingly powerful over water, you're our last hope at curing the spring."

Sir Axis leaned forward, placing his elbow on his knee and his head on his hand. It seemed like he was studying us and trying to decide if we were worthy of saving.

"I can fix your spring."

"You can?" Ciara's voice wobbled.

"Of course, I can fix any water." He lifted his chin and flicked his fingers.

A stream of water flew across the air toward him, landed at the tips of his fingers, and curled up his arm in the same way Ciara's shadows slithered around her arm.

"So, you'll help us?" she asked.

"I suppose I can. Take me to your spring."

Ciara's shoulders slumped. I stepped closer toward her and placed a calming hand on her lower back.

"Only Fae can travel to the Summer Court."

"Such a shame." His brows dipped. "You traveled all this way for nothing. I can't cure the spring from here."

"There has to be a way," she pleaded.

We couldn't have come all this way and be this close to a cure and then have our Veil keep us from curing the spring. I churned the complication over in my head, but I couldn't see a way we'd get Sir Axis through the Veil. Wait... marked mates of Fae could travel through the Veil into the Summer Court, but that would mean Ciara would have to mark him as her mate. I squeezed my eyes shut before snapping them open and staring at Sir Axis. He smirked back at me.

"You recognize a way, don't you?" I asked.

"I'm familiar with the same way you are," he replied.

"No." I shook my head. "Not happening."

"Shouldn't the princess decide?"

"Decide what?" Ciara asked.

I sighed. "Marked mates can travel through the Veil."

Her eyebrows rose then dipped into the biggest scowl I'd ever seen.

"You're not suggesting I mark him as my mate?"

I gulped. "What other way is there?"

She placed her hands on her hips. "After everything we've shared, I can't believe you'd suggest it."

Sir Axis stood. "Don't worry, beautiful, Water Sprites are happy to share. I wouldn't stand between you and your friend spending time together in any way you want."

I narrowed my eyes. "You wanted this all along, didn't you?"

"Me?" He placed a hand on his chest.

His act of innocence didn't fool me.

Ciara tapped her fingers on her hips. "Not saying I would do it, because this idea is ridiculous. If I marked him, then he'd fall into the Quiet for Dia knows how long and he wouldn't be able to help us. So, if he planned this, then it was a flawed plan." She stepped closer to Sir Axis and every part of me wanted to lunge in between them to protect her. "You don't appear dumb enough for that."

"I knew." He stepped the last of the distance between them. "I wanted to see what you'd do. Would you put your happiness first or the lives of your people?"

"That's not what I did!"

"Isn't it? Wasn't your first thought for Malachi?"

She peered wildly over her shoulder at me. My heart clenched inside my chest. This couldn't be her choice. Her happiness over keeping everyone alive. She deserved to be happy. I'd make sure she was.

"It's all right, Ciara," I said. "If I need to share you to keep us all alive, then I will. I'll still love you."

Tears welled in her eyes and her bottom lip quivered. All I wanted was to take her in my arms and keep her safe.

"I'm strong," Sir Axis said. "I'll probably wake without delay from your mark."

She whipped her head back around.

"As soon as I can, we'll go to the Summer Court, and I'll fix your spring." He lifted a hand and tucked the strands of her long hair behind her ear. "The choice is yours, Princess."

CHAPTER TWENTY-FOUR

CIARA

S IR AXIS'S BLAZING BLUE eyes stared into mine. There was a sincerity to the words and the look he was giving me, but his touch made me cringe. I didn't want anyone but Malachi touching me and the thought of marking Sir Axis as my mate sent a swirling nausea to my stomach so harshly, I thought I might vomit. Gulping back the churning nausea, I took a step back. I needed space and distance. My head was telling me this was the only way to fix the spring, but my heart didn't want to be shared with anyone else.

If I marked Sir Axis, we'd be joined forever. He'd see all my memories. He'd learn how much I loved Malachi and for how long. Did it make me a bad princess to want to put myself first?

And Malachi, he was willing to do whatever was needed to save our people yet here I was hesitating.

"You want me to be a part of your harem?" I asked.

Sir Axis smirked. "I'm not a one woman kind of man. No Water Sprites are."

"So, I'd be expected to share you with others?" I'd never imagined marking a mate and having to share them.

"I'll share you too. It's a two-way street. You still want your friend, you can have him."

"Malachi is more than my friend." I huffed. Malachi would always be my best friend, but he was so much more than that.

"Ah, now you admit it."

"There's no point denying it any longer," I said, staring into his striking eyes. "I wouldn't give him up for a mate I'd marked. And I wouldn't even give him up for my fated mate."

Sir Axis chuckled long and low.

"What's so funny?" I snapped as the hairs on the back of my neck bristled to attention.

"You Fae and your fated mates."

I narrowed my eyes. "There's nothing funny about them. They are destined for us. How can you find this humorous? Or are you jealous Water Sprites don't have fated mates?"

"I'm not jealous." He leaned his head closer. "I don't need you so you might as well leave."

Oh, Dia, I'd made a mess of this situation. He was the only one with the power strong enough to fix our spring. I didn't want to anger him. We needed him on our side, but there had to be another way.

"I'm sorry," I said. "This is a lot to take in. I didn't mean to offend you."

His eyes narrowed into slits.

I touched a hand to my forehead. My power surged to my palms and dark shadows seeped from my hands and wrapped around my aching head trying to soothe me.

"Interesting power you have there, Princess," Sir Axis said. "I can't see your head now. You'd make an excellent spy."

I lowered my hands. "Is that what this is about? You want me to be your spy?"

He stalked back to his throne and sat.

Perhaps I was onto something.

"You don't want me to mark you, do you?"

He shrugged looking a little lost instead of the super arrogant man he portrayed.

"What do you want, Sir Axis?" I stepped closer and dropped to my knees. "Because I'll do anything to save my people and my father." My throat closed on the word father, and it came out strangled.

"What is wrong with Fintan?"

I swallowed hard. "He's dying. When the spring slowed, he fed his power into the water to keep it flowing. To keep everyone else alive and now he's exhausted himself." I placed my hands on his knees. "Please, I can't lose my father."

"Oh, sweet child," he murmured then tore his gaze away from me. A worried frown marred his handsome face. "I'll help you, but with the way Earth is now fixing the spring from here is impossible. I need direct access to the water."

"What about access to the water here on Earth?"

"Hmm, that might work. You know where the two worlds connect?"

"Aye," I nodded, hope lighting up inside me there might be a way to fix our spring without me having to mark him as my mate.

"Is the location secure? I won't endanger my people by losing their Master."

"It is very secure," Malachi said stepping beside me and helping me to my feet. "A secret society of humans are dedicated guards of the fountain and to protecting it and the Fae."

"The Fellowship didn't perish when the Trappers attacked?"

"You know of the Fellowship?"

"I know a lot more than you by the looks of it."

"A few Fellowship members survived the Trappers attack and have rebuilt," Malachi said. "And we have King's guards with us."

"With you?" he quirked an eyebrow.

"No, I used my shadows to escape them before coming here. I figured you wouldn't let us in if we arrived with guards."

"You figured correctly." He tapped his fingers on the arm of the throne.

"Plus, my brother and sisters are at the location of the fountain. They'd protect you too, although I'm certain you wouldn't need protection from anyone. You seem exceptionally powerful yourself."

His chest puffed as he drew in a breath and smiled. "You're too smart, Princess Ciara."

"Some days I don't believe I'm smart at all."

"There is one thing you're not smart about," he said standing.

Before I asked what, his arms snapped out, and he yanked me toward him. His lips landed on mine in a kiss that was hard and demanding. I stomped my foot on his instep, he grunted but didn't let me go. He kept his lips on mine as though his life depended on it.

And then the world exploded in a bright ball of light.

CHAPTER TWENTY-FIVE
MALACHI

M Y POWER EXPLODED WITHOUT conscious thought, blasting Sir Axis away from Ciara and onto his throne except the force of the blast kept coming until the throne lay in splinters around him on the ground. Ciara screamed, but my power would never hurt her, so I grasped she was safe, maybe a little shocked but nothing would injure her.

Sir Axis groaned and sat up, streaks of red marred his body and face, and luminous blue swirled around him in waves that seemed to grow in power and intensity.

What had I done?

"You!"

Ciara stepped in front of me. "Don't hurt him."

"Hurt him?" Six Axis all but growled the words. "He planned to hurt me."

"Don't touch her without her permission," I said, easing Ciara to the side so I'd aim my glare at him in full force.

And then Sir Axis laughed while shaking his head. "You foolish Fae. So like your Father and Mother." He jumped to his feet, dusting off splinters and letting them fall to the mess at his feet. "You're all so blind."

Had I ruined our only chance to fix the spring by being overprotective of Ciara? Would he even come with us to the fountain now?

"I'm sorry," I said to Ciara.

She leaned into my side and wrapped her arm around my waist, comforting and supporting me. She was always there for me. Even when I'd messed up. Who would help us now?

"I should punish you. You come into my kingdom and attack me. I should feed you to the Merfolk."

Ciara's shadows swallowed us whole in the blink of an eye. The sensation of her power coating my skin sent shivers dancing over me. Before we'd become lovers, the sensation was one I was accustomed to, one I'd always associated with my friend, but now it was as though her power against my flesh was arousing me and now wasn't the time for me to be turned on by her.

"Brilliant, Princess Ciara." Sir Axis whipped his head back and forth searching us out.

"You won't harm him, ever," she said.

His gaze snapped back to the place where we still stood. "Won't I now?"

"No. You need me and my power for something too, don't you?"

"Like I said, you're too smart." He folded his arms over his chest. "Truce."

"As if we believe you," I scoffed.

"The young man has a point." Sir Axis tapped his fingers on his arms. "How will we trust each other?"

Ciara called her power back and dropped the shadows. "If you don't fix the spring, then I'll die so I won't be able to help you."

"There is that." His blue powers dissipated into the air, floating into the sky and merging with the clouds. "Fine, I won't feed him to the Merfolk."

"You won't harm him ever," Ciara said.

I loved how protective of me she was.

"Yes, yes." He waved his hand in the air.

"You won't kiss me ever again."

He smirked. "Don't say never." He winked.

"I mean it. Even if you can't fix the spring through the fountain and I have to mark you as my mate, then we'll never kiss. Never have sex."

Her words sent even more strength through me I was the one she wanted. That if she'd be able to withstand not being with a man she marked as her mate, then maybe she'd withstand her fated mate when she met him. Maybe she'd always put me first like I hoped.

Sir Axis all but pouted. "You wound my fragile heart, Princess."

"As if you love me," she scoffed.

"Wise, wise, girl." He clicked his fingers and his clothes replaced themselves with new ones and all the cut marks disappeared.

My mouth hung open. I hadn't realized the Water Sprite Master had so much power, but we comprehended little about them. Once we got back to the library, I'd pull whatever books I might find on them and read up on this species of supernatural creatures.

But seeing his display gave me more hope than I ever thought possible. He was the one to cure the spring.

"Well then, let us begin our journey."

"Don't you have people to tell?" Ciara asked.

The young girl rushed from behind a tree and up to Sir Axis's side.

"She'll let everyone know." He patted the top of her head. "Come now."

Sir Axis and the young girl walked along the path into the giant Redwood forest. Ciara and I had no choice but to follow and it wasn't like we wanted to stay in this strange place even if it was the place we'd come together as lovers. I threaded my fingers through hers in the way I always had. Nothing had changed between us, and nothing ever would.

Ciara peered up at me and the expression in her eyes sent my thoughts back to the room we'd shared while she was in heat.

I was foolish to think nothing had changed between us.

Would I have reacted so severely to Sir Axis kissing her before we'd lost our virginity to each other? I wasn't sure and I couldn't test the theory our reaction to each other had changed since we'd had sex because I'd never seen her kiss another man. My power thrummed in my palms. I still wanted to rip him limb from limb for kissing her. For daring to touch her in my presence. I shook my head. This overprotectiveness surging inside me was new.

Sure, I'd always been protective of Ciara, but not to the point it blinded me with rage.

It had to be the spring messing with our powers. There was no other explanation for it.

We stepped between the colossal statues with faces, and I was relieved when no darts shot out of their mouths and into our backs as I'd half expected Sir Axis to go back on his word. In due course, we made it to the entrance of the tunnel, and I flared my power to my hands to light the way, but more to make it light for Ciara so she wouldn't have a panic attack. The lack of talking was getting to me. Until now, Sir Axis was chatty even while keeping everything to himself. Was he worried about entering Earth from his sanctuary? He seemed too powerful to be worried, but I didn't know him at all.

Ciara's father knew him. Which meant he was old, but how old? We couldn't ask King Fintan about Sir Axis since he wasn't awake and lucid.

"After you two," Sir Axis said when we arrived at the end of the tunnel behind the waterfall.

"How do we know you'll follow us down?"

He shrugged. "I guess you don't."

"Enough," Ciara snapped. "Hold hands."

I gripped Sir Axis's wrist in a tight hold. He yanked on his arm, but Ciara's power spread in a thick cloud of shadows, and without delay, Sir Axis clasped the young girl's hand in his as the shadows smothered us all. I'd never seen her cover so many people at once, but she might have with her brothers and sisters. I wasn't with her all the time, I had to remind myself.

"Stay connected otherwise you'll fall down the waterfall."

Sir Axis chuckled. "My dear Princess, you are even more spectacular than I first thought. Are you certain you don't want to mark me as your mate? We'd be unstoppable together."

Ciara shot him a lethal look. "I'm certain. Any other way is preferable to being connected to you."

I laughed, earning me a sharp pain in my hand from where I was holding Sir Axis's wrist. His arm glowed an iridescent blue for a split second and then that too was smothered in shadows. My best friend came to my rescue, and I couldn't love her even more than I did right now.

There was nothing she'd do to make me stop loving her.

CHAPTER TWENTY-SIX

CIARA

"**T**HERE," IVO CALLED OUT. "I heard voices."

"You're hearing things," Emer said.

"I am not."

I stifled a laugh as I kept my shadows around our little group while we climbed down the back of the waterfall. The rocks were slippery with the water, but then the water vanished from the rock face, and they were easier to grip. I assumed Sir Axis used his powers over water to help our descent, but one could never comprehend if he was helping us from the goodness of his heart or to benefit himself.

I thought everything was based on the latter.

"We've been searching for an hour," Emer said. "How would they have disappeared from this enclosed space?"

We descended to the bottom of the waterfall and inched our way along the rock pool beneath. Once we were on the sandy shore, I called back my power and dissolved the shadows covering us.

Ivo and Emer drew their swords.

"Only an hour?" I asked.

"Who are they?" Ivo asked.

"Friends." I flicked them a quick look. "Sort of. They're going to help us cure the spring."

Emer pointed the tip of his sword at Sir Axis. "I don't like the way he's looking at you, Your Highness."

"And in what way might that be?" Sir Axis asked.

Emer stepped closer until the tip of the blade sat below Sir Axis's throat.

"Stand down," I said. "If you kill him, which I doubt a sword would even do, then you'll destroy our only chance at fixing the spring."

"She's smart. You should listen to the Princess," Sir Axis said with his too-smug smile gracing his lips.

Emer hesitated a second then dropped his sword. "Your name?"

"Sir Axis Foxlace, Master of the Water Sprites. You may call me Sir."

"And she is?" Emer pointed at the young girl.

"None of your business," Sir Axis said sounding protective of the young girl.

"In protecting the princess, then whoever is around her is my business." Emer's powers flowed to his palms.

Sir Axis's powers glowed a vibrant blue as he matched my guard's power.

"Princess, I can't believe this." Ivo shook her head. "You disappear for an hour then return with others. One you don't even know her name. What were you thinking?"

"She's a young child and is more timid than a mouse. Her name is Vanya."

"Even mice can bite," Ivo said.

The young girl stepped behind Sir Axis.

"She's relatively harmless for now." He patted her on the head.

"Where did she come from?"

He shrugged.

"Sir, with all due respect, I can't allow the child to be near the princess unless I have more details." Ivo held her ground.

Sir Axis sighed. "If you must know, she arrived from the Spring Court. An old friend found her and brought her to me for safe keeping."

"Who?" I asked.

"Saltine Woodswillow."

I hauled in a startled breath. Sir Axis smirked at my discomposure.

I wanted to slap the smirk from his face. From what I'd read about the Spring Court in books, it was a place many supernatural creatures liked to frequent.

"Does she have any powers?" I asked.

"Telepathy is the only one so far. It's why she's my travel buddy whenever I leave the kingdom." He ruffled her hair this time. "So that I can communicate with my people when I leave."

Jaguar shifters like Sophia, Rian's fated mate, used telepathy between their species and their mates but I had read nothing about them using their minds to communicate with others. I'd read nothing about telepathy being a power for Elves, but then it appeared our library back home was missing a lot of information we didn't know about.

"I suppose that makes her harmless to you," Emer said, but not sounding convinced. "What's the plan?"

"We take Sir Axis back to the fountain and he can use his powers to fix the spring from Earth," I said.

"Try to fix the spring from Earth. With the way Earth is now depleted and your magic hasn't been healing it for many years, I doubt it will work," Sir Axis said.

"It has to work," I ground out, the alternative was not acceptable.

"That's in Ireland," Ivo pointed out. "We're on the other side of Earth in Australia."

Damn it, I hadn't thought of the location. I'd been too focused on trying to make anything else work besides marking Sir Axis as my mate. Would I now have to mark him to take him to Ireland?

The trees rustled, and then Sledge and Arrow burst into the waterfall.

"Who the fuck are they?" Sledge asked with a growl.

Sir Axis rolled his eyes. "Here we go again."

I stepped forward and explained the situation to my sister's mates. They seemed as hopeful as me.

"You'll have to fly in an airplane," Sledge said. "But you'll need identification."

"Fallon's friend would have made them, but he turned crazy, and he's locked up in the Summer Court," Arrow said.

"Well, isn't this getting more interesting," Sir Axis said. "Who is Fallon?"

"My sister, Aislinn's mate," I said offhandedly.

"And these two wolf shifters?"

"What's it matter?" I snapped. "They're my other sister's mates."

"It matters more than you realize young princess."

I glared. "Your cryptic words are giving me a sore head."

He chuckled. "How about some noncryptic words then?"

"Please entertain us."

His laughter grew until he said, "I have a way we can fly there."

"Let me guess, a dragon?"

"Hardly." He rolled his eyes. "Dragons are no longer on this planet. Hmm, that I know of anyway."

I didn't bother asking which planet they were still on. There would be time later once we fixed the spring and my father.

"How?" I asked, not wanting his help but knowing we needed it.

Us Fae hadn't been on Earth long enough to appreciate the ways of the world as it was now.

"Vanya here can use her telepathy to trick humans into thinking our identification is real."

All our gazes landed on the young girl. It appeared her telepathy was more potent than we first thought. Did that mean I should be worried about her joining us? Or should I accept the gift of her powers as a sign we were on the right track to fixing our problems?

"My mother has a clothes shop. You can all get human clothing there to wear on the plane." Sledge pointed at our feet. "And shoes." He shook his head. "You Fae and your no shoes."

I wiggled my bare toes into the soil. "It connects us to our powers. Don't you sense the magical vibrations coming from the soil?"

Sledge shrugged. "Perhaps when I'm in wolf form."

"The Earth is beyond a doubt in trouble," Sir Axis said, bending over and placing his hands in the rock pool of water below the waterfall.

The water suddenly flowed a luminous blue reminding me of his magical home behind the waterfall. Ivo gasped. Emer stared at the water with awe.

The young girl's voice slipped into my mind. "His plans benefit him."

I opened my mouth to ask her what she meant, but Sir Axis snapped his power back and stared at us over his shoulder as though he'd overheard what she'd said to me. His fingers found the medallion around his neck and rubbed the metal.

Whatever his plans were, they included me, so I had to understand them fast because time was running out for all of us. Not only for the Fae King and the Fae but for the humans on Earth too. But how would we save everyone when we couldn't even save ourselves?

CHAPTER TWENTY-SEVEN
MALACHI

THE TREK THROUGH THE forest reminded me of being back home. Branches brushed against our arms and legs as though embracing us into their fold. The sweet scent of the silvery green leaves wafted around us. It marked the place as different from the Summer Court.

"What are these trees?" I asked.

"Eucalyptus," Arrow said. "Native only to Australia."

"They're refreshing." I brushed a hand along a branch and a leaf fell into my palm.

Lifting the leaf, I dangled it in front of Ciara's face letting the aroma fill her senses. She smiled her sweet thank you smile. The one she'd given me many times over the years. I hungered to taste her lips and make her thank me for a different reason. Her cheeks turned a delicate shade of pink as though she'd read my mind before she stared at the surrounding forest.

A pair of birds squawked and flew high into the sky as though we were disturbing their afternoon nap.

"They're so pretty," Ciara said.

"Eastern Rosellas," Arrow said. "They're like us and mate for life."

"Their colors are so vibrant like a rainbow. Are all your birds so pretty?" Ciara asked.

"The native birds are."

"Native?" I asked.

"Not all the birds in Australia originated here. A bit like us others traveled here."

"You don't believe wolf shifters originated in Australia?" I asked.

Arrow frowned. From what Ciara and I had read in the library back home, before the Trappers, the other supernatural creatures had traveled the world unhindered. Had the wolf shifters lost the knowledge? Had we all lost a lot of our knowledge after the Trappers? Perhaps we weren't the only ones who were at a disadvantage with the lack of knowledge at our disposal.

"I hadn't believed so until now..." Arrow stared at Sledge who shrugged.

The path through the forest led us to a quaint town. Houses in varying shades of bricks lined the quiet streets. A few cars chugged along the roads, but most people walked the town square lined with trees bringing the forest into the heart of the town.

"You've made a pleasant home here," I said.

"We have," Sledge said.

"Briana is happy here, isn't she?" Ciara asked.

Sledge smiled. "As happy as she can be considering what's happening in the Summer Court. She's there with your father."

"You didn't go with her?" I asked.

I couldn't imagine leaving my mate for a second and I didn't even have a mate. But Ciara jumped into my mind as the one I'd be leaving and there was no way I wouldn't be by her side.

"Not this time," Sledge said.

"Do you not...?" I shook my head.

"What?"

"I don't know... miss her?" I asked instead of saying, do you not feel like someone has ripped your heart out of your chest whenever she's not with you?

"Of course, I do. What sort of inane question is that?"

Everyone laughed, and I felt like an idiot as heat climbed up my neck.

"I miss her like crazy, but I get she's capable, and she doesn't need me but when she wants me, I'll be there," Sledge said.

Sir Axis chirped up from behind us. "What if she never wants you?"

Sledge glared. "Dude, you have no clue what it means to have a fated mate. To be connected to them in the most intimate of ways. To hold their heart in the safety of yours and for them to do the same."

I almost cheered Sledge for putting the arrogant Water Sprite Master in his place. Instead, I slipped closer to Ciara and squeezed her hand. How would I convey to her I felt that way about her?

Did she feel the same way about me?

Her fingers squeezed mine back.

"We're here," Sledge said opening a glass door and waving us inside. "Be nice to my mother."

We filed into the clothing store and hesitated at the entrance. I, for one, understood nothing about human clothing apart from the ones the Fellowship gave us to wear around their village.

A striking woman stepped from around the counter and looked us up and down.

"Now what strays have you fetched me?" she asked Sledge.

"Ma, this is Briana's sister, Ciara, and her friend Malachi. Her guards Emer and Ivo. Sir Axis and the young girl is Vanya."

His mother's eyes landed on the girl.

"We don't have time for this conversation about who and what they're here for," Sledge said.

His mother's eyes narrowed even further until they were tiny slits staring at us.

"Ma," he pleaded.

"Fine, you'll tell me later," she huffed. "What do you need?"

"They need clothes."

"Yes, I can see. They can't very well go wandering around wearing those lustrous outfits."

"I'll have you know, I have the best garments sewn for my people," Sir Axis said folding his arms over his chest. At least he was wearing a shirt even if he'd left it unbuttoned to his waist.

"Who are your people?"

Sir Axis stepped forward and held out his hand. Sledge's mother placed her hand in his. He raised the back of her hand to his lips and kissed it.

"Sir Axis Foxlace Master of the Water Sprites."

Sledge yanked his mother away. "Keep your slimy hands to yourself."

His mother laughed. "Don't worry, I've met slimier. Besides, I'm happily mated to your father, remember?"

"I'm always happy to share." Sir Axis winked at her.

He'd said the same thing to Ciara and me. Did that mean he said it to everyone, and he hadn't treated us any differently? Were we to be another notch in his long line of bedroom partners? My fingers curled into fists as I struggled to keep my power inside. Sir Axis noticed my struggle and threw Ciara a wink too. She flicked her hair over her shoulder and walked to the closest clothes rack.

I followed her, placing a protective hand on her back. She softened against my touch as though by instinct she realized it was me touching her.

"I can't stand him," she whispered. "If I have to mark him then can I kill him afterward?"

I laughed since I had the same thought myself.

"I'll help."

She lifted her face and studied mine. The slow smile she rewarded me with was worth the way he'd antagonized her. Almost. I never wanted to see her unhappy.

"I wonder how you kill a Water Sprite?" she whispered.

"We'll figure it out. You and I can do anything together."

"True," she said lifting an item of clothing from the rack. "What do you think of this?"

The knitted sweater she held up was striped in a rainbow of colors but compared to the dress she wore, it was hideous.

"Um." I couldn't very well lie to Ciara and tell her it was good. "It's not for you."

"What is for me?" she asked, sliding it back onto the rack and tugging out a deep yellow knitted sweater.

"I like the color it reminds me of you."

"It does?"

"Aye, you're always full of sunshiny optimism."

She laughed and clutched the sweater against her body. "I guess this will do then. Do I get pants or a skirt?"

"Whatever you wear, you'll look stunning."

"Except for the rainbow sweater." She laughed again.

I nodded. "Please, anything but that sweater."

"It might be fun to wear pants." She picked up a pair and held them against her body.

I at once imagined how difficult it would be to have sex with her if she wore pants. Not that she'd said she wanted to have sex with me again. Maybe it was her heat that had made her want me, but I hadn't thought that was the only reason at the time otherwise I never would have caved. I never would have let it be about her heat.

It wasn't like we'd had any time to talk after her heat ended.

"Why are you frowning? Don't you like pants?" she asked.

Snapping out of my wayward thoughts, I said, "It's not that."

"What then?"

I leaned closer and whispered, "I was thinking how much harder it would be to have sex with you if you wore pants."

Her pretty blue and indigo eyes turned to molten heat.

"I'll get a skirt." She shoved the pants back onto the rack and selected a long skirt.

I guess that was the answer to the question I'd been asking myself. Without saying the words, Ciara had told me she wanted to have sex with me again.

"Are you picking something?"

"Sure," I said and strode over to the men's clothing section.

Ignoring Sir Axis, I picked a pair of pants and a shirt then rushed back to Ciara.

"Excuse me...?" Ciara turned to Sledge's mother.

"Marianne," she said.

"Where can we change our clothes?"

"In the back of the shop, there are changing rooms." She pointed to a small, curtained area.

"Thank you," Ciara said.

"My pleasure, sweetheart, we're family now."

Ciara smiled and then walked toward the changing rooms. I chased after her and followed her into the small alcove. There were two rooms on either side of the tiny entry way. Ciara ducked inside one and twitched the curtain closed. I scanned the interior of the shop, noticed no one was paying any attention to us, and then slipped through the curtain Ciara had disappeared behind.

She gasped, her power flared to her palms, but then she raked her gaze over me and dropped them right away. We both took a step toward each other and then we were kissing. There was nothing sweet about it. We ravished each other as though this was our last time together. I wouldn't let that happen even if she had to mark Sir Axis to get him into the Summer Court to fix the spring.

She sighed and dropped her chin to my chest. I wrapped my arms around her back and held onto her. I'd always hold on to her. In this life, however long we had of it, and in wherever we traveled next. She was mine. I was hers. And I didn't need the fates to tell me.

I tilted her chin up and dropped a soft kiss on her forehead. Her eyes glistened, but she nodded. She understood me so well that I didn't have to say the words. I dropped a kiss on her chest over her heart. She gasped delicately.

"Shh." I touched a finger on her lips. "Wolf shifters have exceptional hearing."

She giggled and shoved me away. "You're terrible."

I placed my hands over my heart as though she'd wounded me.

"Go get changed," she said with merriment dancing in her eyes.

Every time I saw a smile on her face it was worth a thousand wolf shifters overhearing us.

CHAPTER TWENTY-EIGHT

CIARA

MALACHI SLIPPED THROUGH THE curtain leaving me alone and I didn't like it. I'd wanted to ask him to stay while I changed out of the magical Water Sprite clothes, but I didn't trust myself to keep my hands to myself if I saw him naked.

I had it bad for Malachi. He was all I thought about when I should think about saving my father, saving the spring, saving every Fae. Then there was Sir Axis... I shuddered. I'd do anything to not mark him. Perhaps I'd go back through the Veil and fetch another Fae to mark him? But with the way our magic was being unpredictable, would I even make it back? It was too risky to try. I suppose there were my guards, but every Fae I knew wanted to wait for their fated mate. I couldn't very well ask anyone else to give up their future happiness to save the Fae.

No, that was all on me as a Fae Princess. All my brothers and sisters had mated except Roisin, and there was no way I'd let her sacrifice her future. It had to be me.

It wasn't like Malachi was my fated mate.

But I chose him.

I'd choose him a thousand times over anyone.

I changed my clothes fast before I flung open the curtain and launched myself into Malachi's welcoming arms. For I realized he'd welcome me. I dashed back out to the shop brushing past Ivo who raised a questioning eyebrow at me. My guards weren't dumb. They'd realize what had happened between Malachi and me. I didn't want to hide it either.

Sledge sidled up to me. "We have good hearing."

I rolled my eyes, and he laughed before walking away. Malachi exited the changing rooms and seeing him in human clothes made me want him even more. They clung to his lean, muscular body in the way I wanted to cling to him. His eyes heated as he walked toward me and everything but him faded away into insignificance.

Marianne cleared her throat. "I have shoes too."

I glared at the offending article of clothing before bending and sliding on the shoes. The moment my feet slid into the soft soles, the connection with my power dwindled. It was as though my powers had become muted. She handed Malachi a pair of shoes too and the moment he put them on, a frown marred his face.

One after another, we all changed clothes until we stood in the shop, appearing more human than ever.

"These clothes are hideous," Sir Axis said while running his fingers over the lapels of his shirt.

Marianne's eyes narrowed to slits as a deep growl rumbled in her throat.

"Sorry," I said. "What I think he means is thank you for your help."

Marianne smiled at me. "You're welcome, dear. But what are we going to do about your charming flower crown?"

I touched my hand to my crown. At least the instant jolt of connection between my powers still happened when I touched the flowers. It comforted me I hadn't lost them in entirety.

"Don't worry about that," Sir Axis said.

"But won't humans be curious at the airport and on the airplane?" Marianne asked.

"Not how we're flying," he said.

"So, you have a dragon?"

"No." He laughed. "I have a magical way to travel. It's how Vanya and I go exploring and keep up with the Earth's events. A leader can't lead properly if they aren't aware of their surroundings."

I placed my hands on my hips. "So, you put us through this for nothing?"

"Not at all." He smirked. "Once we arrive in Ireland, we're bound to encounter humans."

I huffed, but he had a point. The Fellowship had given us human clothes to blend in with the village population.

"So, the thing about Vanya being able to trick humans into thinking our papers are in order?"

"True. It's handy to have her with us."

I dropped my gaze to the girl, but unlike last time she filtered nothing into my mind. A deep sigh left my chest. Why couldn't everything be easy?

"Sorry, wolves," Sir Axis said. "You'll have to stay here. I can't have everyone knowing all my secrets."

Sledge squared up to the Water Sprite.

"I don't like you," Sledge said.

Sir Axis chuckled and rolled his eyes. "Alphas."

"If you hurt one hair on any of their heads, then I'll rip your body limb from limb and if that doesn't kill you, I'll keep the parts separate so you'll never be whole again."

Dia, it was good to see my sister's mate was protective. He'd protect her with his life as all mates should.

I hugged Sledge. "I'm glad Briana has you."

He squeezed me back with his beefy arms.

I hugged Arrow next. "Give Saoirse and Ailbhe a hug from me."

"I will," he said gruffly.

I turned to Marianne and embraced her too. "Thank you for your help today."

She patted my cheek. "Family."

I nodded. Our family was growing, and it should have been a time to celebrate. Instead, the weight of our impending demise overwhelmed us.

"I suppose you comprehend the way?" Malachi asked Sir Axis.

"Of course, you don't think I hide around these parts and not appreciate what's going on, do you?"

"No," he said.

I slid my hand into Malachi's and followed Sir Axis and the girl back through the town and into the forest with my guards taking up the position behind us. Each step made my insides quiver with excitement and nervousness. I'd never flown before and didn't grasp what to expect since I'd only just left the Summer Court.

"How do water sprites fly?" I asked.

"I don't actually fly," Sir Axis said. "I use my magic to travel through the water particles. Similar to your Veil except I can travel anywhere there is water whereas your magical portal is between Earth and the Summer Court. My people can travel anywhere at any time."

"You're taking us to Ireland with magic?" Malachi asked.

"Of course."

"Can't we meet you there then?" Malachi asked.

I didn't like the idea of Sir Axis using magic on us either. He'd already given us a magical potion that was more than what he'd told us and now he wanted us to trust him to take us on his magic.

"I think that's a good idea," I said. "We'll go through the Veil, and you can meet us there."

"Where? Ireland is a big place. You wouldn't want me to get lost and lose even more time, would you?" Sir Axis drawled.

I sighed. "So, help me if this is like the potion... I'll..."

"Yes?" He cocked an eyebrow.

He understood we needed him to fix our spring more than anything including my fear he'd do something else to us. The added threat from Sledge should have been a deterrent to Sir Axis, but I sensed he wouldn't care about an alpha wolf shifter.

He held a branch aside, and we stepped onto the sandy soil surrounding a glistening lake. The water stretched across the land until a row of trees appeared in the distance. It reminded me of how our lake back home used to look before the spring slowed. Before everything started to go wrong. Was he going to use his magic to travel through the lake?

"All right, I concede. You can travel through the Veil, and Vanya and I will meet you there."

"How will you find us?" Malachi asked.

Sir Axis lifted the medallion from his neck and slid it over his head. He stepped closer to me. "Wear this and I'll find you wherever you are."

I stepped forward. He lifted the chain over my head and settled it on the back of my neck. The medallion was heavy and warm against my chest. My fingers rubbed the metal the way I'd seen Sir Axis do.

"What is it?"

"Mine, that's all you need to know."

"So long as this doesn't make me yours now." I let go of the medallion.

Tiny vibrations of magical power emanated from it.

Sir Axis winked, then turned to Vanya. "Hop on."

Vanya jumped on his back and wrapped her little arms around his neck.

"Of you go then. We can't find you if you don't leave."

I called on the Veil, sensing the magical disturbance with our powers made it even harder to manipulate the lock. Shadows danced from my hands and coated the air in front of our faces. Time ticked as I turned with the magic and sprung open the Veil.

"I'm trusting you," I said to Sir Axis.

He dipped his head, and Vanya smiled over his shoulder. Surely, if a young girl liked the arrogant Master, then he couldn't be totally bad?

My guards walked into the swirling, dark, magical curtain. Clasping Malachi's hand, I stepped into the Veil. Hoping I hadn't read Sir Axis wrong. Hoping he'd find me with his medallion.

CHAPTER TWENTY-NINE
MALACHI

"**W**E'RE BACK HERE AGAIN?" I asked, taking in the caravans.

"I figured it would be a good place to meet up with Sir Axis and Vanya," Ciara said. "It's far enough away from the village that it's discreet for our travel through the Veil." She let out a long breath. "Besides, we don't know if Sir Axis needs discretion as well."

"How long do you think we'll have to wait?" Ivo asked.

"I didn't think to ask him that." Ciara's shoulders slumped.

"Why don't you and Malachi wait inside a caravan?" Emer said.

"I'm fine out here," Ciara said.

"It's safer," Emer insisted.

Was she giving us a chance to be alone? I'd take it with both hands.

"I agree." I nudged Ciara gently toward the caravan.

Her gaze flickered to me then the caravan, and suddenly she was walking toward it with hurried footsteps. I followed her. She was the love of my life. I'd follow her anywhere she went. We climbed the timber steps and stepped inside the cozy caravan. A small bench seat in earthy tones sat on one side, while on the other was an assortment of kitchen cabinets. At the back of the caravan was a large bed decorated in more earthy tones of soft browns and greens, as though the bed was made from the surrounding forest, except made from plush cushions and blankets. I longed to see Ciara spread across the bed, satisfied from the pleasure I'd given her. I locked the door behind me. Not that a flimsy human lock was a match for supernatural creatures, but so Ciara knew I didn't want us to be disturbed. Because I'd take this moment alone and make it all about us.

"I despise seeing his medallion around your neck."

Ciara lifted it in her fingers. "It's a strange piece of jewelry. I'll take it off."

She raised the chain higher, but it stopped at her chin as though an invisible force wouldn't let her remove it.

"I guess I can't."

I nodded. I'd suspected there'd be a magical quality to the charm around her neck. Sir Axis didn't do anything without a reason.

"Now what do we do?" Ciara asked.

A smile stretched my lips. I imagined a million sexual fantasies I'd had over the years. We might have a short time, or we might have a long time to wait in the caravan. Either way, we'd have a pleasurable time while waiting.

I stepped closer to Ciara and brushed her hair over her shoulders. Tiny goose bumps lifted on her arms.

"There is one thing we could do..."

An answering smile graced her pretty lips. "And what might that be?"

My fingers toyed with the strands of her hair. "I think you know."

She giggled. "Ivo and Emer will hear us."

"I can be quiet."

She laughed again. "I'm not sure I can be."

"Hmm." I raised my hand and placed it over her mouth. "Would this work?"

Her luminous blue and indigo rimmed eyes widened, but she nodded her head against my palm. I shifted my hand out of the way so I could kiss her. And kiss her, I did. I devoured her like she was my last breath, and I couldn't breathe without her. It was true. I couldn't imagine life without her. No matter what, she would always be the woman I loved and even if Sir Axis's medallion never left her neck, then she'd still be a part of me.

Ciara's hands slid over my shoulders and across my back, drawing me closer to her. I kept my distance and tugged the top of her dress down. Her breasts spilled free, and my eager hands cupped her tender flesh. A moan rippled out of her throat.

Dammit, she probably wouldn't be quiet enough, so her guards didn't hear us and know exactly what we were doing in here, but I figured Emer had sent us inside for this very reason.

"Shh," I whispered.

Ciara giggled. "See, this won't work."

"It will."

I glanced around the tiny caravan. There. I found what I needed. A circular hanger held an assortment of scarves. I stepped around Ciara and stroked each scarf, looking for the softest material to use on her.

She tugged her dress back up and settled on the bed with a disgruntled humph.

I chuckled and made my way over to her, carrying a silky scarf in a vibrant yellow.

"Dress back down."

Her eyes widened. "I thought..." her pale pink tongue darted out to her lips.

"You thought wrong," I said. "I'm going to love you and show you how much you mean to me, even though you're wearing *his* medallion."

Ciara glanced at the medallion, then tugged the top of the dress down once again freeing her breasts. The rosy peaks of her nipples hardened in an instant. I crawled across the top of her. Her breath quickened. I loved how much my presence affected her.

"Do you trust me?"

"Always." She nodded.

"I'm going to tie this around your mouth."

"Oh." She gasped.

"Yes?"

"Yes. I want you. Now. Hurry."

I didn't waste time because we might not have much alone time together.

"Open," I said.

She opened her mouth, and I slipped the fabric past her lips and tied the ends at the back of her head.

"Are you all right?"

She nodded her head. I placed a soft kiss on her parted lips. The material taste mixed with the usual pleasant taste of her, but it only made me want her more. I ran my tongue down her neck to the peaks of her nipples. There I swirled my tongue around each one until they both glistened with moisture and peaked into delightful buds. Her moans were muffled through the gag as she lifted her legs and tried to wrap them around my waist.

I stroked my hands up her legs under the folds of the dress. Her hips rose to meet my fingers as I found her core already slick with arousal. A deeper moan muffled through her gag, but I couldn't stop even if Sir Axis was already here. There was only our pleasure at this moment.

My fingers parted her, and I slipped two inside her warm heat, reveling at the way she was ready for me in an instant. Maybe I wasn't the only one who was full of lustful thoughts for my best friend. Her hips rocked back and forth in time with my fingers. Her walls tightened. She was close to orgasm, but I wanted us to be together.

I slid my fingers free and popped the buttons on my pants. My hard cock sprang free as though on a mission of its own. Not waiting a moment longer, I covered Ciara's body with mine. My cock rubbed against her swollen flesh then slid inside her. She let out another muffled moan while I bit my lip to keep from moaning myself with how good she felt.

Keeping quiet was harder than I thought it would be.

That thought fled as instinct took over and our bodies moved in unison. My cock thrusting hard into her. The medallion warmed between our chests. I almost imagined it was Ciara's power marking me as her mate, but it wasn't. I thrust into her harder, wanting to make her mine in every way.

Her fingers dug into my shoulders as every muscle in her body tightened, and then she came with a muffled cry against the gag. The strength of her orgasm sent me over the edge. There was nothing better than giving her pleasure, feeling her pleasure, and knowing I was the one who made her this happy.

I rolled us over with my cock still buried deep, not wanting to leave her. My fingers found the knot in the gag and released it. She lifted her head and smiled, a satisfied grin on my face.

Her lips parted as though she was about to say something, but then a knock pounded on the door.

"They're here," Emer called out through the timber door.

"Coming," Ciara yelled back, then placed her hand over her mouth to smother her giggle.

I kissed the back of her hand and helped her climb off me. She smoothed the ruffles of her skirt back into place while I tugged the top back over her breasts. Then her fingers were at the buttons on my pants and doing them up for me. I patted down a few stray strands of her hair and stroked a flower on her crown. She shivered and smiled.

"Well?" she asked.

"What?"

"Do I look presentable?"

"You'd look presentable in a brown bag."

She reached up and placed a quick kiss on my lips. I gathered the gag and stuffed it in my pocket.

"Memento." I shrugged.

She smiled and strode toward the door, more composed than I was. I suppose she was raised as a royal princess, whereas I wasn't. My hand reached for the lock and opened the door. She swept down the stairs.

Sir Axis stared at her as she walked toward him. Neither of us had voiced our concern that he wouldn't even come, but that niggling thought had been in my head, so I was sure Ciara had thought it too.

"Take it off," Ciara said, lifting the medallion. "You found us, so take it off."

Sir Axis grinned. "So prickly Princess. Who ruffled your feathers? Or should I say dress?" He winked and stared at me.

My power surged to my hands, but I struggled against the jealous rage pounding inside me.

He laughed as he reached for the medallion. His fingers closed around it, then he lifted it over Ciara's head and returned it to his. The medallion shone as it hit his skin.

"Mmm, delicious," he purred.

"Enough," Ciara said, walking back to my side. "Time for you to make good on your word."

"As you wish, Princess." He dipped his head.

Ciara clasped my hand in hers.

Ivo stepped in front of us and led the way even though we'd been here in this town a short time ago. I guess she was on alert. I didn't blame her after all the things we'd dealt with since coming to Earth. Our change of clothing was even more of a waste of time, and I hated Sir Axis a bit for not saying sooner we were using magical means to travel.

A few drunk men staggered along the streets. But if we'd still been in the Water Sprite clothing, then they wouldn't have mattered. They were too drunk to care, and if they did, then no one would have believed them if they'd seen strange people wearing clothes that glowed.

The golden streetlights lit our way along the cobblestone streets until we arrived at the vine-covered wall surrounding the library.

"Interesting," Sir Axis said.

"What is?" I asked.

"The magical barrier surrounding this place." He lifted a hand and tested what must have been the barrier.

The solid timber door clicked open, and a man appeared holding a lantern. The golden light shone on all our faces.

"Princess Ciara, we're glad to have you back," the man said.

I recognized him, but I couldn't recall his name. It was terrible of me we'd studied the books alongside the

Fellowship and yet I hadn't become friends with them. Not that I didn't want to. It was the sensation of the ticking clock counting down the death of our spring and the Fae.

"Can you gather everyone?" Ciara asked. "We have news. Exciting news."

The man's gaze ran over all of us again. "You've brought a stranger with you."

"Aye," Ciara said. "An exceedingly powerful one. I'll explain once we're safe inside."

"And he's to be trusted?" he asked.

Which was what I wanted to know, too. Could we trust Sir Axis?

"He's the only one who can help us," Ciara said instead.

The man's lips firmed, but he let us inside the walls and hurried to find the others while we walked through the thick, overgrown vegetation. Sir Axis tutted under his breath as though letting the place become a shambles was a grave error. The man was more complicated than anyone I'd ever met. True, I'd spent most of my life with only Fae, but we were a varied bunch.

We arrived at the fountain and halted at the edge. We knew better than to touch the water, but Sir Axis stepped closer as though the magic drew him to the running stream falling over the stones and disappearing beneath the moss-covered rocks.

"Fascinating," he mumbled, stretching a hand for the water.

"Don't touch the water," Alister's deep, gruff voice emanated from behind us.

The entire Fellowship stood behind him, and so did Aislinn, Fallon, Pepper, Lorcan, Roisin, and the Fae King's guards. They were a formidable force with their powers and the swords held in their hands. Would Sir Axis take them all on? Or was he more of a team player than I gave him credit for?

"But it's what they brought me here for," Sir Axis said.

"Be that as it may, you can't walk into our most sacred place and think to touch the sacred water."

Sir Axis huffed and crossed his arms. "Fine, I won't fix the Spring of Life then."

Alister's eyes narrowed. "You can fix the spring? The fountain and all that is wrong with our worlds?"

"Hardly." Sir Axis laughed. "But it'll be a start."

Ciara tilted her head. "I'm not sure I understand."

Sir Axis sighed and held up his hands. "Two worlds joined by powerful magic." He intertwined his fingers. "They used to look like this." Then he bit by bit unraveled his fingers. "Now they're more like this."

"We depend on each other," Roisin said.

She was always smarter than we gave her credit for. Most saw her as the artist, but her senses were attuned to the smallest details, so why wouldn't she have noticed what we'd failed to see?

"Separating the Summer Court from Earth caused our problems?"

Sir Axis said nothing, which made the hairs on the back of my neck stand on end.

"Who is he?" Alister asked.

Ciara told everyone who Sir Axis was, how he would help us with his powerful water magic, and why we'd brought him here. If our two worlds were still connected enough, then he'd be able to fix our spring through the fountain. If not, then she'd have to mark him as her mate to take him into the Summer Court to fix it there. Aislinn gasped when she said that, but she didn't realize the worst of it. Ciara and I loved each other more than best friends. Or that we'd joined our bodies as one. We were as close as we could be without marking each other as mates, and we didn't need to mark each other to learn the other's memories since we were always together. Our memories were already joined. I offered her my silent support by stroking her lower back. Each stroke eased the tension running through her body and I was glad I could do that for her, even if I couldn't fix the problems facing us.

Alister rubbed the back of his neck once Ciara finished talking.

"I suppose it's worth a try, but if you damage the fountain, your head will leave your body," Alister said.

"Touche, old man," Sir Axis dipped his head before plunging both hands into the fountain.

Ciara gripped my arm hard, digging her fingertips into my skin, but I'd take the momentary discomfort for her, because if this failed then she'd mark Sir Axis as her mate, leaving me with no chance of being the one for her.

Luminescent blue flared from his hands and rolled over his body in rippling waves of water as though he, too, was made from the fluid. The entire fountain glowed from the wall behind it to the cobblestones underneath and even the green moss turned blue. The sight was spectacular and while I didn't like Sir Axis, I had to give him credit for how powerful he was. Long moments passed, and glowing blue droplets of sweat rolled down his forehead as though what he was doing was a great strain on him.

"It's no good," he said, his arms vibrating in the water. "I can't get through the Veil to the other side."

Then the blue exploded in a large flare, knocking us all from our feet. Glowing blue droplets landed at our feet before rolling back toward the fountain as though the magic of the water was calling it all back together.

"Shite," I muttered.

Ciara rolled her head toward me as we lay on the ground. The absolute devastation in her eyes broke my heart.

CHAPTER THIRTY

CIARA

"No," I SOBBED. I'D put everything on this working and now...

I sprang to my feet and ran through the garden. The tangled mess of the overgrown plants tore at my clothes and skin beneath. The human shoes were atrocious. I kicked them off and the connection with my powers flared with more force than I'd ever experienced. Shadows danced from my palms and over my forearms, and more and more engulfed me with every step I took. I dashed down the steps of the underground library and along the first aisle where I cowered at the end of the row of books.

I'd thought I could do it. Put my happiness aside for the sake of my father and our people, but every limb shook. This wasn't right. Nothing about marking Sir Axis felt right.

There had to be another way. I grabbed the nearest book and laid it on the floor in front of me. The words were blurry through the tears in my eyes, but I forced myself to focus on them. To find another way.

"Ciara?" Aislinn called. "Are you in here?"

I bit my lip. There was nothing Aislinn could do to help me except study the books.

"She'll be here," Roisin said. "She loves books. They're her comfort."

Bloody sisters understood me too well.

"I'm here," I croaked out through the tightness in my throat.

Footsteps grew closer until they almost stepped on me.

"Stop," I cried. "You'll damage the book."

"Dia, forbid we damage a book." Aislinn rolled her eyes.

"Or our sister," Roisin said, kneeling on the floor mere inches from the book. "We can't see you. How about you drop the shadows?"

My bottom lip quivered. "I don't think I can."

"We're not letting you mark someone who's not your fated mate," Aislinn said.

"But it's the only way to get Sir Axis into the Summer Court to fix the spring."

"No. Not happening," Aislinn said.

I loved her take no shite attitude.

Roisin's hand crept through the shadows and touched the book. "I found a book, so I'll find you."

I let out a strangled laugh. My power became less insistent on protecting me and bit by bit the shadows drew back until they disappeared.

"There she is," Pepper said. "Pretty cool power by the way."

"Thank you," I said to my sister-in-law. "Do you have a potion or something that would get Sir Axis through the Veil?"

She tipped the cloak from her head. "Not that I know of, but I'll double-check my spell book."

"I'd appreciate that," I said, snapping the book shut and standing.

"I'm with your sisters here. You can't mark someone who is not your fated mate."

"But witches don't have fated mates."

She shrugged. "But I understand how much it means to your brother to have me. I saw his memories of you. And Malachi... are you sure he's not your fated mate?"

"What?" Aislinn asked. "They're best friends. Aren't you, Ciara?"

My cheeks warmed so much it was as though the sun was blazing down on them.

"Oh, do tell." Roisin rubbed her hands together.

I shrugged, then smiled remembering all the things we'd done to each other.

"We, ah, had sex."

"What!" Aislinn screeched. "When?"

"I fell into heat while we were away."

"You're pregnant too?" Roisin asked.

"No. Sir Axis gave me a contraceptive potion."

"Why would he do that?" Aislinn asked.

"We were at a ball. All the Water Sprites drink them before they have their orgies."

Pepper cackled. Aislinn appeared appalled, and Roisin giggled.

"You were at an orgy too?" Aislinn asked.

I heaved out a sigh. "We left the ball once it started."

She slid a dagger from a holster and twirled it around her fingers. "What is Sir Axis up to?"

I shrugged. "He seems to think I'll help him with something using my powers and that's why he's helping us."

"At least we recognize he's not here by the goodness of his heart," Aislinn said.

"He and father were friends, so I think he wants to help him."

"Back to you and Malachi," Pepper said. "Are you certain?"

"Aye," Roisin said. "What about you and Malachi? Do you love him?"

"Of course, I love him. I've always loved him."

"But now you've had sex, do you love him more?" she asked.

Did I? Was it possible to love him more than I already did? I tossed the question through my heart instead of my mind. It comprehended the answer to the question.

"I love him so much more I can't imagine loving anyone else more. I can't imagine not having him in my life. If I lost him, then I'd die from a broken heart." I heaved out a long sigh.

"Sounds like the way I feel about Fallon," Aislinn said. "Maybe Pepper is right. What if Malachi is your fated mate?"

"Why wouldn't I have known?"

Aislinn shrugged. "The moment I met Fallon I comprehended they fated him to be mine. What if because you met so young you didn't realize what the sensation meant?"

"Perhaps."

"Plus, Lorcan didn't realize the feelings he was having for me meant I was his fated mate," Pepper said. "Men can be clueless sometimes."

"True," Aislinn said. "Although Saoirse didn't realize Arrow was her fated mate because she was in heat."

"I think the spring's decline is messing with everything," Roisin said. "I couldn't think of a better man for you than Malachi. He makes you so happy."

"He's my best friend."

"You make him happy too," Roisin said with more wisdom than most fifty-year-old Fae. "We had to stop him chasing after you."

"Why would you do that?" I gasped.

"See you want him more than anyone," Pepper said.

I frowned. Was Malachi my fated mate? Had he been all this time? What if they were right?

"How do I comprehend for sure he's my fated mate?"

"Your powers will tell you," Aislinn said. "They'll make you want to mark him."

Dia, ever since we'd had sex that was all my powers wanted to do. I'd struggled to keep them from overwhelming me. But did I dare believe we were fated?

"But our powers aren't right with the way the spring is now. We have to fix the spring."

"We do." Aislinn placed a calming hand on my shoulder. "And we will. We'll get the Water Sprite into the Summer Court another way."

"How?"

"I'm not sure yet, but we'll think of something. We'll find it in this library. In these books." She nodded as though she was right.

"We don't have time. Father..." I gulped. "Doesn't have time."

"At least let us search for a day?" Roisin pleaded.

I couldn't say no to my little sister. She was father's favorite and if she was willing to make father wait another day to be healed, then there had to be hope.

"Ciara?" Malachi's voice called out.

"I'm surprised he waited this long," Roisin said.

"Me too," Aislinn said.

"You made him wait to see how long he'd stay away?" I fought the smile trying to form on my lips.

"Aye fated mates can't stand to be apart," Aislinn said.

"You should see Lorcan." Pepper rolled her eyes but smiled while doing it. "It's like I can't even pee in peace."

We all laughed, easing the tension of the moment. Malachi's footsteps emanated down the stairs and then he walked down the aisle.

"Are you all, right?" he asked, his gaze settling on my face.

I drank in the sight of him letting the relief at being near him settle the pain I'd had in my heart. Perhaps they were right, and Malachi was my fated mate all along.

"I am now you're here," I said.

One by one they hugged me and left us alone in the library.

"We'll keep everyone out for as long as we can while you two talk, but we'll have to get back to researching soon," Aislinn said.

"Research?" Malachi asked.

"Aye. We're not letting Ciara mark Sir Axis," she said.

His shoulders sagged as they walked past him.

"I don't know whether to be happy or concerned," he said.

"About?"

"You not marking him." He scowled as though the idea of my mark on another man made him angry.

"I'm both," I said. "I understand if you're feeling both too."

One side of his lips tipped up into a smile.

"Ciara..."

"Wait. My sisters think..."

"Think what?" He stepped closer.

The comfort I always experienced in his presence grew. Hope blossomed inside my heart.

"They think we might be fated mates," I whispered scarcely daring to say the words I hoped were true.

"What?" he croaked out the word.

CHAPTER THIRTY-ONE
MALACHI

T EARS GLISTENED IN CIARA'S hopeful eyes. I drew her into my arms and kissed her forehead letting my lips linger then slide to the corner of her eyes to kiss the salty liquid seeping from them.

"Don't cry," I whispered. "Every tear you shed is like a blade to my heart."

"But what if they're right?" She lifted her chin. "What if we've wasted years of happiness together as fated mates because we were too dumb to realize?"

"One," I said. "We're not dumb." I rubbed my lips over the curve of her jaw. "Two we've been happy together for years. Being your friend has been an honor and a privilege. No one makes me smile the way you do. No one makes me laugh the way you do. You light up my life, Ciara. You always have and you always will."

I lowered my lips to her mouth and caught her soft gasp. She clung to me as I kissed her tenderly reinforcing with my lips the words I'd poured from my heart. I believed every word I said. She'd made me happy. Happier than any woman would ever make me simply by being my friend and if now we experienced the added benefits of sexual pleasure with each other then that was a bonus.

Breaking the kiss I never wanted to end, I said, "I love you no matter what, whether you're truly my fated mate."

She sobbed and then buried her head into my chest. Her hands clung to me as if I'd leave her.

"I'll never leave you," I whispered. "Never stop loving you."

"Malachi." She hiccupped. "Kiss me. Love me."

"With pleasure." I brushed my lips over the sensitive curve of her shoulder, reveling in the shivers dancing over her body. Higher up her neck I let them wander until I found the soft lobe of her ear and suckled it into my mouth.

"I love you. Only you," she said lifting her face. "I want you to be my fated mate more than anything in the world."

"Then we will be."

She smiled. "So now we're making up the rules?"

"You and me together can do anything." I caught her face between my palms. "Besides, we can rewrite the rules in new books if we want to."

She laughed huskily then stood on her tiptoes to meet me in another kiss. This one wasn't sweet. This kiss was full of the passion we'd found. The desire we'd a short time ago let come to light. Her mouth drifted over mine swallowing my groans of appreciation for the woman she was, for the princess who tried her best to help everyone but herself. This time though it was all about her and I'd show her how much she meant to me.

I found the bottom of her sweatshirt and slid my hands beneath it over the silky soft skin of her stomach and higher to the swell of her breast. Goose bumps rippled over the soft curves as my fingers stroked and teased until I found the hard tip of her nipple. She moaned into my mouth as I brushed over the peak. And when I squeezed the tip between my thumb and forefinger, she arched into me pressing her breast into my palm. I needed more of her like this. My other hand joined the first under her sweatshirt teasing and stroking her breasts until her kiss turned erratic and she wrenched her head away.

"Take it off," she demanded.

I peered over my shoulder. "Someone might see you and I don't want anyone to see you but me. You're mine, Ciara as I am yours."

Her eyes twinkled with mischief and then her powers exploded in a sudden cloud of darkness covering the both of us.

"There, now no one will see either of us." She grinned.

"Dia, did I tell you how much I love you?"

"Aye but tell me again."

"I love you more than anything in this world and the Summer Court."

"Make love to me?"

"You never have to ask me for that. I'll gladly make love to you whenever and wherever you want me to."

I drew the sweatshirt over her head and tossed it on the floor. Her rosy-tipped breasts begged me to suck on them and so I did. First one tight nipple then the other until they were glistening with my saliva and Ciara was moaning and clutching at my hair.

"Now," she said fumbling for the zipper on my pants.

She wrenched it down and then wrapped her hand around my hard cock. Her palm was like sweet heaven, and I thrust into the soft grip making my legs shake with need for her and only her. Regaining some of my senses, I drew her skirt up her legs until my hand brushed her bare thigh. Dia, I loved skirts and dresses. In particular Ciara in them. She whimpered as my fingers teased the tender flesh of her inner thigh before finding her slick core.

"So wet for me."

"Only you," she whispered.

"Only me," I agreed.

"And this is only for me." She tightened her grip on my cock and drew me closer toward her dripping entrance.

"Always and forever."

She rubbed the tip over her eager flesh. I lifted her leg exposing the treasure that was all mine. Every piece of Ciara was mine to treasure. She'd offered me everything she was, and I'd hold her treasure deep in my heart until the day I died even if the day would be sooner than either of us wanted. But I wouldn't let those dark thoughts into this magical moment.

My power flared in my hands as I thrust into her, sealing us together as the way we should always be. She shuddered at the instant connection between us. Perhaps we were fated mates. I doubted this sensation happened with all sexual encounters. I wouldn't know since she was my first and last. My everything.

I caught her hips in my hands and lifted her higher. She wrapped her legs around my waist, and I stepped forward until her back met the wall of the library. Her hands wrapped around my neck then her lips slammed into mine. We kissed frantically as I pumped my hips into her slick core. Her inner muscles tightened and stroked my cock with each long, deep thrust until we were both quivering. Both of us were poised for the explosion of pleasure between us.

My power urged me to mark her. To seal us together then no one else could have her. My hand lifted to her chest, but I couldn't do it when... groaning I shifted my hand higher, so it curved around the soft skin of her delicate neck. She shuddered, and I drew back a fraction to see the blinding lust raging in her eyes. I watched her face as I held her against the wall. As I pumped my hips harder into her, making her mine. Her body drew tight. Fingers clamped around her neck. Her legs squeezed my hips. There was no better sensation than right here with Ciara watching her pleasure peak and come undone.

With the next thrust, I tightened my hold on her neck, and she exploded into the freefall of her orgasm. The tight clenching of her inner muscles almost made me topple over the edge with her, but I kept pumping into her, kept the magic of this moment alive for Ciara as long as possible until my balls tightened, and my cock strained for release.

"Mine," she whispered.

That one word made me come undone. I exploded deep inside her, shuddering with the force of my orgasm. Each jerk of my cock sent pleasure so acute to every inch of my body that I didn't want it to end.

Voices echoed down the stairs. Loud voices.

"Shite." I yanked out of Ciara, dropped a quick kiss on her lips then gathered up her discarded sweatshirt.

"Ciara, Malachi?" Pepper's loud voice echoed through the library.

They were getting closer, but Ciara's shadows still engulfed us. I fixed my clothing, then watched Ciara fix her clothing. Pepper and Lorcan stood at the end of the aisle.

"We left them down here," Pepper said.

"I don't see them," Lorcan said. "They must have left."

Ciara laughed making Lorcan and Pepper peer down the aisle.

"She must be using her shadows," Lorcan said. "Come on out, you can't hide forever."

"I can if I want to," Ciara said.

"Well, if you don't want to hear about the potion Pepper found," Lorcan drawled.

"What potion?" Ciara dissolved the shadows.

Their gazes roamed over our rumpled clothes, Lorcan's eyebrows lifted while Pepper grinned.

"Did you two have sex?" Lorcan asked.

"So, what if we did?" Ciara placed her hands on her hips.

Pepper cackled. "Oh, you're as bad as Lorcan. You two have to be fated mates."

"What?" Lorcan asked.

"Don't you see it?" Pepper asked.

Lorcan's brows twitched down, then rose again. "You might be right."

"I'm always right," Pepper said.

"What's the potion?" I asked because as much as I wanted Ciara to be my fated mate, we still had the problem with the spring to face.

CHAPTER THIRTY-TWO
CIARA

"IT'S NOT ONE I'D let anyone use under any other circumstances, but desperate times call for desperate measures, right?" Pepper said.

"I suppose..."

The tone of her voice made me hesitant to learn what she was talking about.

"I can make a chameleon potion," Pepper said.

"What does that mean?" Malachi asked.

"It's a dual-acting potion so two people need to drink it. When you do, you swap physical appearances," Pepper said. "I'm hopeful it would be enough to get Sir Axis through the Veil."

"The Veil wouldn't fall for a trick like that," I said. "Its magic is too powerful."

"Maybe," Pepper said. "But the Veil's power is erratic now like everyone else's. In theory, it should work."

"And if it doesn't?" Malachi asked.

Pepper shrugged. "You understand the workings of the Veil more than me."

"The magic might be as simple as stopping the person from crossing through," Ciara said. "It might be more volatile though, but I've never heard of the Veil injuring a person."

"It's worth a shot. We have nothing to lose by trying," Lorcan said. "That's if you're willing?"

Malachi clenched his jaw. "You want me to swap appearances with Sir Axis, don't you?"

"No," I said, cringing at the idea of Malachi looking like Sir Axis.

"Sir Axis has already agreed to try," Pepper said.

"Of course, he has," Malachi said. "He wants Ciara."

"He won't get her," Pepper said. "This is a better idea than her marking him."

"So, we're all agreed then," Lorcan said. "We'll try Pepper's potion."

Malachi ground his jaw but nodded his head.

I grabbed his arm. "You don't have to do this."

"I do. I don't like it, but I do."

The determined set of his jaw and the way he stared at me made me realize there was nothing I could say to him to stop him from drinking the potion. In a matter of minutes, he'd no longer look like himself and Sir Axis would look like him.

"How long will the potion last?" I asked.

"A few hours. Long enough to get Sir Axis into the Summer Court," Pepper said.

"I'm only trusting you because you're Lorcan's mate."

Pepper stepped closer to me and said, "I would never harm your family. You're my family too now." She touched a hand against her chest where Lorcan would have placed his mating mark. "All I've ever wanted was to be loved for who I am not despised for who I am. Your brother gave me that and I'd never jeopardize Lorcan's love."

I sniffed because the heartfelt way she'd said those words made me remember what else was at stake. It wasn't only about me and Malachi. There was Lorcan and Pepper. My other brother Rian, his fated mate Sophia, and her entire jaguar shifter colony. My sisters Briana, Saoirse, and her baby, plus their wolf shifter mates. If I failed to fix the spring, then we'd lose everyone important to us.

I lunged and hugged Pepper. She didn't hug me back for a few seconds and then she did. It was an awkward hug, but we'd perfect it in the years to come.

"I'm ready."

We walked up the stairs and found Sir Axis waiting at the top with the Fellowship. They must not have wanted him in their sacred library, and I didn't blame them.

"Ah, Princess Ciara, are you here to take me to the Summer Court?"

"Aye," I said holding back the rage simmering inside me when I realized he'd soon look like the man I loved.

"Your witch seems to think a potion will work."

"It might," I said, holding onto the small bit of hope that would never die in me.

"This should be fun." Sir Axis grinned.

I stepped closer toward him and poked a finger into his chest. "I'll still comprehend it's you."

"Will you?" he cocked an eyebrow in the cocky way he always did.

"Aye."

"We'll see." He leaned closer and whispered so only I heard. "Maybe you'll mark me instead of him."

"Never." I stomped away from him and over to my sisters.

His grin never dropped as Pepper motioned Malachi forward. She drew two vials from her pouch. I guess she'd had time to make them while Malachi and I had been in the library having sex. I should be guilty for taking the precious time away from our quest, but I'd never be guilty about loving Malachi.

Malachi gazed at me once before turning back to Sir Axis. They drank the potions together then Pepper uttered a spell. Magic drifted into the air. Tiny particles rose above their heads. The magic shifted colors as each word left Pepper's mouth. When she finished, the particles dropped from the air and onto their heads. Their bodies shimmered out of focus and no matter how hard I stared, blinked, and squinted, I couldn't make out who was who. As the magic dissipated it revealed Sir Axis and Malachi standing in opposite places.

"Malachi?"

Malachi who now appeared like Sir Axis turned his head toward me. I staggered back a step placing a hand on my racing heart.

"I'm still me," Malachi said still sounding like himself.

I nodded, but I hated every second of looking at Malachi and seeing Sir Axis.

"Sir Axis," I said shoving the pain away and stepping away from the gathered group of people. "Take my hand and let's go."

Sir Axis, looking like Malachi, walked over to me with his confident swagger. It wasn't the way Malachi walked, so I recognized it wasn't him. Would this trick the Veil even though I could tell the difference between the two? We were about to find out. Emer and Ivo stood behind me ready to protect my back. Sir Axis took my hand, and he felt nothing like Malachi.

"This will not work," I muttered under my breath before reaching for the Veil.

The magic of the Veil pulsed in the air. It surged and retreated as though struggling to form beneath my power. I threw more power into my hand which turned dark with my shadows. In due course, the Veil gave to the raw royal power coursing through my body. I almost smiled in triumph, but this wasn't my best friend by my side holding my hand.

I stepped into the Veil tugging Sir Axis with me, but the second his body hit the magic, it didn't let him through.

"No." I tugged on his hand, but it was like trying to drag him through a brick wall. "It's not working."

"Shit," Pepper said.

My power throbbed nonstop inside me. My head hurt, but my heart hurt even more. At least Malachi would only look like Sir Axis for a few hours. At least Pepper's potion failing wasn't permanent. Like if I'd marked Sir

Axis as my mate. That was permanent. The idea of marking someone other than Malachi sent my power into a raging fit. Shadows shot out everywhere engulfing Sir Axis and he fell through the Veil and landed at my feet shrouded in my darkness.

"Oh my god," Pepper said. "Her powerful shadows engulf others. They become a part of her. Why didn't I think of that when I saw her in the library?"

As the Veil shimmered, ready to slam shut, Malachi called out, "You can do this!"

At least his voice was still the same even if my last vision of him wasn't how he should look. I shook my head and clasped Sir Axis's hand tight because if I let go, he'd become lost in the Veil. And now, I almost had him in the Summer Court. Almost had him close enough to fix the Spring of Life.

I wouldn't let go for anything.

CHAPTER THIRTY-THREE
MALACHI

"**W**HAT HAVE I DONE?**" I stormed over to the fading Veil. "I can't let her go by herself. I'm always by her side. She's my best friend. I should be with her for this."

"She's a big girl," Pepper said.

"I love her. I need to be with her." I turned to Lorcan, whom I'd known forever. "Take me through the Veil, please."

"I don't want to risk it until the potion wears off."

"Damn it," I threw my hands up in the air surprised when an explosion of my power burst into the sky in a bright radiant white light.

The Fellowship gasped and made a lot of noise as my power lit up the sky then faded into the distance.

I held my palms out to the Veil, but the magic wouldn't give for me since I wasn't a Fae royal. I couldn't unlock what the King had put in place and the doorway wasn't working. They'd stranded me here looking like Sir Axis until the potion wore off.

Then I'd go after Ciara.

My best friend.

The woman I loved.

Every ounce in my body said she was mine.

I believed it now.

She was my fated mate.

CHAPTER THIRTY-FOUR
CIARA

T HE VEIL PARTED IN the woods near the palace, which was a strange place for us to exit, but it meant we were closer to the spring than if we'd come out by the tower Father had built to contain the doorway. The doorway was useless now anyway, but when Sir Axis fixed the spring, then it would work again. Then Malachi would use it to come home to me.

"This way." I tugged Sir Axis's hand forcing my shadows to disappear.

"My dear, if you were in such a hurry to get me to your bedchambers then all you had to do was say so," Sir Axis drawled.

"I don't care if you look like Malachi, I'd never have sex with you."

I let go of his hand trusting Emer and Ivo would make sure he followed me. It wasn't like he could go anywhere. He was stuck inside the Summer Court now and the only way for Sir Axis to get back to Earth and his people was to help us.

Ivo stepped beside me and whispered, "I'm so happy to hear about you and Malachi."

I jolted. "You are?"

"Aye, you're perfect for each other." She fell back and walked beside Sir Axis.

The palace rose high in a sparkling enchanted display of beauty. It always took my breath away that I lived in such a magical palace.

"I almost forgot how beautiful this place was," Sir Axis said.

Startled I spun around. "You've been here before?"

"Yes, many, many years ago. When your great-grandfather was King of the Fae. His death was such a tragedy by that evil Siren."

"All deaths are a tragedy," I said.

"Touche."

As we walked closer to the palace, I expected Grier to open the door and usher us inside, but he didn't appear like he usually did. Were we too late? I rushed up to the door, but Emer beat me to it and opened the heavy timber pushing it inside the quiet palace.

"Where is everyone?" I asked glancing left and right.

"The spring, Your Highness," Emer said reminding me of our mission.

"Aye."

I sped through the marble hallways of the palace deeper into the heart until we entered the atrium. The place was usually full of an abundance of fluffy white blooms hanging from the ceiling, but now the flowers were brown, the plants hanging limp as though struggling for life. A sickly yellow moss-covered the rocks. The slow trickle of the spring sent panic through every inch of my body. Each step was like knives slicing my skin.

Shoving back the thoughts of my father, for I couldn't bear to think he might already be dead, I motioned Sir Axis over to the water.

"Fix it, please," I pleaded.

Inch by inch as though time meant nothing to him, Sir Axis walked to the edge of the spring. His hands disappeared into the water as though the water swallowed them whole and ate them. Was it too late? Had everything been for nothing? My throat closed over. Would I die now not having marked Malachi as mine while in the presence of a man who appeared like him but wasn't him?

"Please," I croaked.

Sir Axis turned and winked at me before his hands glowed a luminous blue lighting up the entire atrium in an ethereal glow. The water turned a vibrant blue. The rocks beneath shone blue. Even the dying plants turned blue. Did I look blue too? Sir Axis wasn't blue. I peered at Emer and Ivo and they weren't blue either. Whatever Sir Axis was doing, it only affected the spring and its surroundings.

He mumbled under his breath as time stretched while he worked his magic. By degrees, the trickle of the spring grew faster. Even more slowly, the strength of the spring intensified. Breathing became easier as the fear that had a choke hold on me eased. The Water Sprite Master was fixing our spring. I'd hoped he would, but I'd never expected he could. I'd thought something had doomed us even though I'd pretended I was certain we'd find a cure. I hadn't been certain.

My hand searched for my best friend who was always by my side, but right now when I wanted to share the wonder of the spring coming back to life, he wasn't here. He wasn't with me to share in this joyous moment. Pain flared in my heart so intense I staggered to the nearest boulder and sat heavily.

Sir Axis stared at me, his form wavered in and out of focus and then he was him again, but now the sight of him wasn't unwelcome. He'd saved us.

"Thank you," I said pushing the word out through my tight throat filled with emotion.

He winked and turned back to the spring. His power didn't stop fixing our ailments. Soon the blue eased back from the flowering blooms revealing them in their fluffy whiteness once more. Then the blue faded from the rocks and the water leaving them clear to the eye. The water flowed so forcefully I sensed it in every part of my Fae being he'd fixed it.

Sir Axis stood with a flourish and held his hand out to me. I placed my palm in his and let him haul me to my feet.

"You did it," I said with awe.

"I'm offended you didn't think I could fix my mistake." He placed my palm against his chest. "How about a thank you kiss at least?"

"Could and would are two very different things." I squished my lips together. "What do you mean by your mistake?"

"A slip of the tongue."

"From what I've seen of you, you don't make mistakes."

"Ah, sweet princess."

"Tell me now." I tugged on my hand, but he held it steadfast against his chest.

"I merely wanted your father to come out of hiding. I didn't expect this plan of Saltine's to go to this extreme."

"Saltine? What does she have to do with our spring?"

"She did nothing to your spring."

"So it was you! You tricked me into believing you were helping us when you were the one who caused the problem to start with."

"There is more at stake here."

CHAPTER THIRTY-FIVE

MALACHI

"Now, now, now," I said the moment my body shifted shape.

Every second away from Ciara was a second too long. Lorcan reached for the Veil, and it sprang to life beneath his glowing palm with ease. Did that mean he was stronger than Ciara, or had Sir Axis fixed the spring? I wanted to hope it was the latter.

Lorcan grinned as though he sensed it was the latter.

"Take me to her."

I didn't need to tell him twice. We stepped into the Veil, and he closed it at once as soon as Pepper was by his side. Where a fated mate should be. Where my fated mate should be. Ciara was mine.

The Veil parted in the atrium and the scene before my eyes made me angry. I stormed across the cobblestones and pushed between Sir Axis and Ciara.

"Don't touch her," I growled the words while facing him.

He rolled his eyes. "Fae fated mates are such a pain in the ass. All this don't touch her. Relax. She was only going to give me a thank you kiss."

My fist flew at his jaw before I even registered I was going to punch him. Ciara grabbed my arm and hauled me back. Sir Axis worked his jaw side to side.

"Like I said, don't touch her," I gritted out through clenched teeth.

"Yeah, yeah." Sir Axis waved us away. "Now I've helped you, it's your turn to help me."

"I realized you weren't doing this out of the goodness of your heart."

"I have plenty of goodness in my heart." He folded his arms over his chest.

"You're the one who caused the problem. Why would we help you?" Ciara said.

"What?" I growled.

"A good friend of mine, Saltine Woodswillow, can predict the future, so when she tells me to do something, I do it."

"No questions asked?"

"Of course, I ask questions, I'm not stupid." He sneered. "There are good reasons why I altered your spring to get your father to leave the Summer Court. She never predicted the way the connected magic had become warped to turn it into this big of a problem."

"Unfortunately, I believe him. Saltine used to be our witch seer." Ciara leaned over my shoulder. "How can we help?"

"You need to convince the King to lift the lock on the Veil. To connect the two worlds as they once were. The Fae need to come back to Earth and rule," Sir Axis said. "To fix Earth too."

Ciara's hair brushed my arm as she shook her head. "That might be impossible."

"Impossible but necessary." He waved to the spring. "Even without my influence, the spring will languish again if you keep the two worlds apart and this will have all been for nothing."

"What else do you want from Ciara?"

He smirked. "When the young girl Vanya reaches adulthood, I need her to help me return her to the Spring Court."

"It's a two-for-one deal. Wherever Ciara goes, I go." I folded my arms.

"Obviously." He rolled his eyes. "But it's Ciara's shadows I need."

"Why do you need shadows to return the girl?" Ciara asked. "Did you steal her?"

"I would never do such a thing."

Sir Axis appeared offended.

"Then why?"

"She's special. The Elves like special things. I'm protecting her until she can find her future fated mate in the Spring Court."

"Why?"

"Because I'm a good guy." He shrugged. "Because Saltine's visions need me to."

Was he a good guy? He might have been an asshole to us, but he'd helped us. Perhaps he wasn't as bad as I thought he was. If he was only trying to get the Fae King to lift the lock on the Veil and reconnect Earth and the Summer Court as they once were for the greater good, could we be angry with him? And I knew from stories that the King had held Saltine in great stead. The expression on Lorcan's face said he believed him too.

"Now, who's taking me back to Vanya?"

"I will," Lorcan said. "I trust Saltine's visions. She helped Father and I defeat the Trappers. She wouldn't have orchestrated this without good reason."

"We will," Pepper said.

And there was the love of fated mates staring me in the face. It was the same love and devotion Ciara and I had. All this time they had fated us to be together and we'd been too close to see it. Well, I wasn't too close now. Now the spring was flowing, our future was brighter, and we had time to mark each other as fated mates.

My power throbbed in my palms.

I couldn't wait to mark her as mine.

But more than that, I couldn't wait for Ciara to mark me as hers.

CHAPTER THIRTY-SIX
CIARA

"**I** NEED TO SEE Father," I said, tugging on Malachi's arm.

When he'd swooped in all heroic telling Sir Axis not to touch me, it'd made my heart flutter. Not that I wouldn't have stopped another man from touching me, but there was the way Malachi made me feel as though he'd take on anything for me. It was a heady sensation to realize there was one person in the entire realm destined for me. And that person was Malachi.

He was mine.

I was his.

Forever.

Malachi nodded and wrapped an arm around my shoulders. I dismissed Emer and Ivo now we were in the safety of the Summer Court. They both appeared as relieved as me the spring was once again flowing fast even if we had one more thing to do to fix it permanently. I'd convince Father, we all would.

Our lives were about to change, but they needed to. We couldn't hide away in our utopia forever when everywhere was suffering because of it.

The long marble hallways were still empty which made me fear we were too late to save Father, but the solid strength of Malachi by my side kept hope alive. I tugged at the human clothes, wishing to take them off more than ever. The material was itchy and added to the stress of not knowing if Father was still alive. My steps quickened. Malachi kept pace beside me.

Faster and faster, I walked until I broke into a run. Malachi ran with me. He didn't tell me to stop. He supported me in everything I did. I loved him for it even more. We raced around the corner and skidded to a stop before my parents' bedchambers.

I knocked, waiting for an answer. Grier opened the door, took one look at us, and ushered us in.

"He's..." His voice cracked.

I thought the worst. Father had died. Mother's crying filled the room making me think it even more, but then Grier stepped aside.

Father sat upright in the bed hugging Mother to his chest while she cried. It was the best night of my life. My father was alive.

"Father?" I gulped past the lump in my throat.

His head whipped my way. "Ciara? The spring... I sense it running well again."

I nodded. "It is."

"She fixed it," Malachi said.

"I'm glad you figured it out." Father smiled.

"I didn't." I shook my head. "The Water Sprite Master fixed it for us, but he said it's only temporary. You need to unlock the Veil otherwise it'll happen again."

"Sir Axis?" Father asked.

"Aye."

Mother sat up straight. "He helped us?"

"He did," Malachi said. "But he had a hand in our problems too."

"I'm not sure I understand," Father said.

"He said it was because of a vision Saltine had, that he tried to get you to leave the Summer Court and reunite the two realms," I said.

"Saltine? We owe him a debt of gratitude if he was acting on her visions," Father said.

"I owe him a debt," I said.

"No, this is my fault," Father said throwing back the covers and standing. "I'll talk to Sir Axis."

"You'll have to go to Earth," Malachi said.

Father gazed at Mother, then nodded his head. "The family has much to discuss, and we will, but right now, I need time alone with my mate."

"We understand," Malachi said.

I backed out of the doorway with Malachi by my side as always. Mother's pain-filled words drifted to us, "I thought I'd lost you."

I couldn't imagine the pain she must have suffered feeling like that. The idea of losing Malachi when I hadn't even marked him sent a sharp stabbing sensation through my body. We strolled through the hallways, the relief running through my body so intense I headed toward my bedchambers so I could lie down.

Malachi paused outside my door.

I clasped his hand in mine and hauled him into the confines of my bedchambers.

He laughed. "It looks like a library in here."

I grinned. "I know your room looks the same."

He smiled then took me in his arms and led me toward the bed. "I believe it."

"What?"

"We're fated mates."

"I do too." I climbed onto the mattress and tugged him with me.

"For two smart Fae we sure were dumb," he said climbing over the top of me.

"I couldn't agree more," I said, unbuttoning his shirt and shoving it from his body. "I never want to wear human clothes again."

"Me either," he said sliding his hand under the sweatshirt and urging me up so he could draw it over my head. "Were you attracted to Sir Axis while he looked like me?"

I shook my head wildly. "No, I recognized in my heart it wasn't you, and you are the only one I want."

"You're the only one I want, too."

"So..." I trailed my fingers over his chest.

"Aye," he said. "Mark me as yours. I want your memories even though I understand you already. I want to appreciate you even more. And I want the world to realize I'm yours. I want every woman to recognize I'm yours. Every man too."

I laughed. "Mark me too."

"I thought you'd never ask." He sighed.

We kissed with the love we had for each other, with the love we'd always have for each other. It was branding, deep, and full of the desire we'd always had for each other but were too scared to admit. We were no longer scared. Malachi and I appreciated we had love. We realized we'd love forever too.

There was no better emotion than knowing you had a fated mate.

Our hands tugged the rest of the human clothes free from our bodies and we caressed and stroked. Loved and pleasured until there was only us in this room. There was only the connection fated mates experienced when they were with each other. We'd always been together, so we had known no difference that we'd already found what others searched for.

I wouldn't think back to what if we'd known sooner. There was only here and the future. A future that would spread with many possibilities. I was certain Father would do the right thing. Certain Mother would make sure she didn't lose her mate because I'd do the same to save Malachi. Knowing I'd found a love like my parents made me happy. It'd make them happy too once we told them and we would as soon as we woke from the Quiet because marking Malachi was too important to not do right this minute.

My power flared to my palms, as did Malachi's, but we kept caressing each other, marking the other with our power in a different way than the mating mark. Malachi's power tingled against my skin making my core hot and slick with need. Every touch of my power over his skin intensified the sensation tenfold as though I'd sense how much my touch turned him on.

He rolled us over and guided my core to his straining cock. I slid onto him gasping at the sensation of fullness, of rightness, filling my body. My power surged more than it ever had and as I rocked my hips on top of his. My palms drifted to his chest needing to mark him. To make him mine.

Malachi's hand pressed against my chest. The white brightness of his power lit the room chasing away my shadows and made me realize what was in front of my face my entire life. I might be dark, but I'd never be the darkness when I had Malachi as my fated mate. He grounded me. Loved me. I loved him too.

As our hips thrust faster, our powers flared harder. The building orgasm rocked through our bodies at the same time as the power took over marking us. Darkness filled my vision as Malachi's memories swarmed into my mind.

The first thing I saw was me.

The second thing I saw was Malachi smile at me.

Our fate had been there right from our first meeting.

I slumped against his chest letting the Quiet take me under into the depths of Malachi's memories. He would see the same as me. He'd see the love I had for him all my life. I was glad he'd see how much I loved him because words would never describe the way I felt for Malachi.

And when we woke from the Quiet, we'd spend eternity showing each other the passionate desire we'd hidden for so long.

We'd show each other and everyone else fated mates could do anything together.

We'd fix both worlds.

FATED MATES OF THE FAE ROYALS

1. Fae's Song

2. Fae's Wolf

3. Fae's Alpha

4. Fae's Heart

5. Fae's Witch

6. Fae's Dream

7. Fae's Fate

8. Fae's Love

Acknowledgments

First, thank you to my family for putting up with me disappearing into the world of books. To Belinda, thank you for encouraging me to write again after I lost everything in a computer crash. Remember to back up! A lot of work goes into creating a story, and I'm always thankful for the support of my online writing buddies, beta readers, and fellow authors, Immy for always making me smile, Tammy for believing in me from the start, Karen for being willing to read any level of heat I write. Cassie for her hand holding. Lana for her invaluable knowledge. Also, my fabulous beta reader Erica and her help with US English. The biggest thank you goes to my 'twin' Dannielle, who is the best critique partner, cheerleader, and sounding board ever, and is forever fixing my comma errors, sorry Dannielle I'm afraid you're stuck with them and me. Finally thank you to all you romance readers. You are my tribe.

ALSO BY

Anthologies

Reluctant Bride

Alpha Male

ABOUT AUTHOR

Helen Walton is a tea drinking, chocoholic, romance writer. Stories are her obsession. She adores creating sensual romances containing a sprinkling of humor and the all-important happy ending. She lives in South Australia with her family, and menagerie of quirky animals where they all take her away from her book world and demand to be fed. Lucky for them, she enjoys cooking but prefers baking.

Sign up for my newsletter for exclusive content.

https://www.helenwaltonauthor.com/newsletter

Visit my website

https://www.helenwaltonauthor.com/

Follow me

BB bookbub.com/profile/helen-walton

f facebook.com/Helen-Walton-Author-103496667706602/

g goodreads.com/author/show/20249188.Helen_Walton

⊡ instagram.com/helen.walton.author

♪ tiktok.com/@helen.walton.author